REMEDIES FOR ENEMIES

MAGIC & MISDEMEANOURS 1

R.A. LINDO

PERIUM PUBLISHING

Copyright © 2021 by R.A. Lindo

All rights reserved.

No part of this book may be reproduced in any form or by any electronic or mechanical means, including information storage and retrieval systems, without written permission from the author, except for the use of brief quotations in a book review.

CONTENTS

Author's Note	v
Welcome to a Magical Universe	vii
1. New Beginnings	1
2. Wizarding Rules	9
3. Touching the Sky	18
4. Sparks of Sorcery	26
5. Above Ground Antics	36
6. Tonic for Trouble	46
7. Mercurial Learning	58
8. Society Trials	70
9. Quiet Time	81
10. Prizes & Preparations	91
11. Shifting Targets	100
12. Tell Tale Signs	110
13. Lessons in Loyalty	118
14. The Illustrated Quarter	130
15. The Art of Alchemy	139
16. Wise Guides	152
17. Witches' Brew	160
18. Close Call	169
19. Judgement Day	177
20. Friendships Forged	186
Teaser Chapter Book 2	195
About the Author	205
Also by R.A. Lindo	207

AUTHOR'S NOTE

Magic & Misdemeanours is a spin-off series, following a character from the **Kaira Renn Series** and **The Fire Witch Chronicles**.

There's no need to read the two previous series, but please be aware there are some references to them in the **Magic & Misdemeanours** series.

WELCOME TO A MAGICAL UNIVERSE

Welcome to the secret, magical universe of **The S.P.M.A. (The Society for the Preservation of Magical Artefacts.)**

If you want to delve deeper into the magical universe of the S.P.M.A., **sign up** to become eligible for free books, private giveaways and early notification of new releases.

You can also join **my private Facebook group** where all things S.P.M.A. are discussed.

Founders' Quad Map

Society Square Map

1
NEW BEGINNINGS

The classroom buzzed with excitement as the eight students enjoyed all things magical.

"Comeuppance," Leah Creswell said, laughing at the sight of an object appearing in the pocket of her jeans.

Taking out the oval object, Leah threw it in the air above Olin Zucklewick's head, causing the small, diminutive boy-wizard to sway in all directions. The Ozzer was one of the many artefacts they'd learnt about, Leah being lucky to win it in their last assessment.

Looking like a white pebble, it caused the intended target to lose their balance, making it impossible for them to regain a static position: the sort of thing likely to come in handy when their above-ground assessments began.

Above-ground was the non-magical world they were born in, knowing nothing about the S.P.M.A. until a year ago, when a well-dressed brother and sister paid a visit to their homes: Casper and Philomeena Renn.

The students were terrified of the duo who ran The Cendryll, knowing they were two magicians you *definitely* didn't mess with. Casper and Philomeena could do *unbeliev-*

able things ... things the class could only dream of at the moment ... but that could all change if they proved themselves worthy of a life in the Society for the Preservation of Magical Artefacts (S.P.M.A. for short).

Using a charm to generate light from their fingertips, Ethan Lyell and Tom Koll turned the wisps of light into swords, feigning battle before their teacher arrived. Although he'd been accepted by his classmates, Tom was still struggling to find his feet in a group destined for potential greatness.

The nephew of an infamous wizard, Tom felt the burden of his past more than the others, although they all had crosses to bear. As Ethan and Tom's friendly sword fight continued, Katie Follygrin looked on from her seated position by one of the stained-glass windows, watching Ethan with a mixture of love and longing.

The other girls shared a knowing glance, aware any teasing of Katie would lead to a backlash — a girl so focused on winning she'd lost sight of the power of friendship.

"Are you going to be this annoying *all* day?" Ava Blin asked, the tallest of the group decorating the ceiling with a shower of light.

"Until our teacher turns up," Tom replied, ducking to avoid Ethan's sword swipe.

"So mature," Tilly Flint commented, the girl whose fire-red hair matched her temper.

"So boring," Ethan countered sarcastically, patting his immaculate afro hair. "We're in a *secret, magical Society* and all you do is sit there and sulk."

"Maybe I didn't choose to be here."

"Then maybe you should leave. No one's forcing you to stay."

"It's not that simple."

"Isn't it?" Olin prompted, deciding to create a waterfall to stand in: a way of reminding Tilly of the once-in-a-lifetime opportunity they'd been given.

"It doesn't matter," Tilly added before taking out a small, circular notebook. Flipping it open, she rubbed the letter 'A' on the first page, whispering something before an intricate illustration formed. Staring at the illustration, Tilly sat cross-legged on the floor, studying the buildings forming in the picture.

"Looks like someone's having second thoughts," Ethan whispered to Tom as he turned his sword into a lasso of light, whipping it around his friend's legs until he hung upside down in the makeshift classroom — just as their teacher appeared through a portal of light: Jacob Grayling.

"Morning," came the quiet voice of Jacob, glancing up at Tom's suspended figure. "Well done for volunteering, Tom," their young teacher added, sipping a yellow remedy they were desperate to try.

"*Sir*," Tom moaned, knowing what this meant: he'd 'volunteered' himself for the first task.

Jacob was the perfect teacher, Tom thought: kind, caring, funny and committed to his role as guardian of The Fateful Eight (the name given to the eight students chosen by each magical faculty). He was also a Society legend, having survived two wars in as many years. Tom hoped he could experience battle when he was older, assuming he made the cut.

First, he had to survive being the target of this morning's lesson. As he hung in mid air, glaring at Ethan who offered him a sarcastic wink, the day's lessons began with the appearance of familiar company: beautiful, luminous insects fluttering in through the holes in the walls ... insects known as Quij. The delicate insects floated towards each desk, resting on the edge like a magical mascot.

No *actual* furniture decorated the room, the desks and chairs formed from a simple creative charm. In fact, it didn't look like a classroom at all, but that was partly the point. Magic was infinite in its potential, something Jacob was tasked with teaching The Fateful Eight. With light streaming in from the small holes in the walls, it was time for the wizarding to begin.

"THE ART OF VANISHING IS HARDER THAN IT LOOKS," JACOB began, perched on a stool of steel, "and it's the skill we're going to learn later today."

"*Yes*," Ethan whispered, his handsome features and charm making Katie secretly swoon.

Standing off the stool, Jacob clicked his fingers to turn the stool into a whistle: a simple trick of transforming steel into any object imaginable: an artefact known as a Vaspyl.

"Who knows what the three vanishing charms are?"

All hands went up, desperate to earn points towards their final score and the chance of permanent magical living.

"Olin," Jacob said, pointing to the small, astute boy sat at the front of the class.

"The Disira charm, Verum Veras charm and a portable Perium."

"And the portable Perium is known as a …?"

"*Cympgus*," Ava blurted out — her tall, athletic figure giving her an advantage in physical assessments. "Any Society door acts as a portal transporting you elsewhere, but a Cympgus comes in handy when you need to disappear above ground: portable transportation."

"And the Verum Veras charm stops you from ...?" Jacob prompted, pointing to Leah Creswell who seemed eternally happy.

"Being seen," Leah replied with a beaming smile. "It generates a curtain of sparkling light, keeping you hidden from above-ground eyes. You activate the Verum Veras charm before disappearing from view."

"And if you make the mistake of being seen?"

"You get kicked out with your memory wiped," Tom replied from his suspended position in the room, bringing a smile from the others.

"Good to know you're still with us, Tom," Jacob teased. "Better still, you're in the perfect position to act as a target."

"A what, sir?"

"A target, Tom. *Remedies for Enemies* has been the topic of this term, and morphing steel is a particularly effective remedy."

The colour drained from Tom's face at the thought of steel objects flying in his direction — a thought shared with the other students who wondered if their gifted teacher was joking: he wasn't.

"Vaspyls out," Jacob instructed, throwing the silver whistle into the air ... a whistle that transformed into a flute which he placed into his mouth. "Soon, your lessons will take place in real time, meaning you need to know how to get out of sticky situations. Morphing steel comes in handy if you happen to bump into some unsavoury characters, *stunning* them being the aim."

"Very funny," Tilly commented, studying the bright-blue Quij resting on the edge of her desk. "As if you're going to hurt Tom."

"Stun," Jacob reinforced with a smile, shooting silver darts at Tom who yelled in fear. Realising this was a trick, the suspended student looked up to see a circle of dots on the ceiling.

"*Hilarious*," Tilly added sarcastically, offering a feigned gesture of surprise.

The surprise turned to shock when the silver dots shimmered into spikes, darting towards the seven students stationed at their desks ... their training kicking in as steel objects transformed into protective cells ... the darts bouncing off the impenetrable steel.

With the daggers retreating to dots, and Tom released from his suspended position, The Fateful Eight sat in stunned silence, staring at the teacher they'd always viewed as gentle and kind. He was suddenly on edge, sipping his yellow remedy as he rubbed his temples: a sign things were about to get more serious.

"Before we get on to the skill of vanishing, we need to master the art of defence — both will be tested when you go above ground."

"I thought using magic above ground was banned?" Roan Khan queried, his painfully thin frame looking like it could break at any minute.

"It is, without express permission," Jacob explained, "but it's time to extend your wizarding skills. Ultimately, this is a trial to see if children can be trusted with an incredible secret. Those that can will remain in this universe of wonder."

"Have you seen it all?" Ethan asked, trying to trip Tom up as he walked past. "Every magical realm, I mean?"

"A lifetime wouldn't be enough to experience it all," Jacob replied as the Quij rested on his shoulders: the tall, young teacher with legends in his family, "but if you survive these trials, you'll have a lifetime of discovery ahead of you."

"I hope I make it," Leah stated, looking dreamily at The Cendryll skylight visible through the holes in the walls: The Cendryll being the name of the magical faculty they were linked to. "To know you lived in a world where *everything meant something*, every doorway led somewhere and every object contained a magical mystery. I don't know what I'll do if I fail."

"Go back to normal," Katie said with a roll of the eyes, ever the competitive spirit.

"As if it's as simple as that," Roan Khan countered, the boy with an ambition to become a Society soldier.

"Well, it *is as simple as that* because our memories will be altered," Katie replied,

"But the residue will remain," Olin suggested, casting his shrewd eyes over the others. "Like a whisper from the past, tugging at a memory we can't form."

"Residue or no residue, we'll be stuffed if we fail, returning to normal school and normal living," Ava added, "so it comes down to who's good enough."

With the small class pondering their forthcoming trials, Jacob studied the wall recently smashed by a lost boy turned king: Taeia Renn. He remembered how quickly Taeia's gifts had been ignited, sparking war in the sky realms.

He didn't sense danger in his students, but knew all too well the perils of magical living, making him wonder who'd be the first to fall foul of Society laws. He enjoyed their innocent wonder, secretly hoping they all proved themselves worthy of Society living. Magical living took its toll, though, something the young witches and wizards would soon learn.

"We learn the brilliance of morphing steel this morning, then onto the art of vanishing in your favourite game."

"Rucklz!" the class said in unison, jumping out of their chairs at the thought of blasting through portals of time on The Hallowed Lawn.

As the students chose teams, forming the expected groupings, their young teacher looked on, his Society tie worn loosely. On the surface, he looked like any other man in his early twenties, but Jacob Grayling was far from ordinary.

The brother of Guppy Grayling — the legendary Fire Witch — he had seen things most people could barely imagine, travelled to realms beyond dreams and witnessed death at every turn. Society living was spectacular living but it came at a cost: a price The Fateful Eight would have to pay to make the grade.

"Right, get ready to improve your mental dexterity," Jacob stated, moving between the luminous desks and chairs, a silver cane spinning in his hand. "Your remedy is your Vaspyl; the enemy is whatever I release from *this*."

Thoughts of Rucklz faded at the sight of another silver artefact ... a circular object punctured with holes ... ready to release whatever creature their young teacher chose.

With each student sitting upright at their desks of light — steel objects grasped tightly in their hand — the morning's wizarding began as Jacob flicked open the lid on the silver contraption, releasing an ear-piercing scream to send a shudder through young bones.

2
WIZARDING RULES

The ear-piercing scream was followed by a blizzard of black ... black birds that screeched towards their target. The shock was almost too much for Tilly Flint who dropped her Vaspyl ... the steel ball transforming into a triangular chamber that she scampered within, just in the nick of time.

The other students responded with the expected speed of wit, transforming morphing steel into prisms, squares and oblong shells — all acting as protection from vampiric birds known as the Ameedis. Of course, Jacob had no intention of releasing the birds on his class, but they didn't know that and were responding as if their lives were in danger.

A yelp of fear was released from Tom Koll as the Ameedis smashed into his steel prism ... a co-ordinated attack that made it seem like they were under Jacob's control ... which, of course, they were. A Zombul had the power to release and *control* any creature the user could imagine: a visit from vampiric birds the order of the day.

The Ameedis were legendary for their viciousness, typically located in the stench-filled realm of Dyil's Ditch: a wasteland of screaming buildings few made it back from. Thankfully for the class, Jacob had done battle with far worse creatures, looking on calmly as the black birds swarmed around his students' protective cells.

"Can you call them off!" Ava Blin yelled from her oval-shaped cell. "They're screeching is *awful*."

"Their bites are worse," Jacob quipped, deciding to explode the creatures into dust.

With dust filling the room, the class stepped out from their steel cells, Roan and Olin looking the calmest of the group. The others appeared shell-shocked, as if it had only just dawned on them that magic wasn't all fun and games.

"What's got into *you* this morning?" Ethan asked, containing a rage that sometimes got the better of him. "You *know* we're not ready to be attacked."

"Who said anything about being attacked?" Jacob challenged his mixed-race protege. "The Zombul controls everything released from it; it was a test of mental dexterity."

"By setting a vicious creature on us?" Katie Follygrin countered, tying her blonde hair into a ponytail as her competitive spirit kicked in. "We're *kids*, for God's sake."

"I thought you wanted to be witches and wizards."

"We do."

"Then stop moaning," Jacob replied, spinning a steel cane as the protective shelters remained in place. "You're the lucky few deemed worthy of wizardom. You're *tasting* it, *touching* it but that's all it is at the moment: a simulation of the real thing. If those creatures weren't under my control, you'd all be dead.

If the blades weren't designed to miss you, you'd be lying in pools of blood. Remember, this is an experiment, allowing eight children into our secret universe. Eight children from each faculty, multiplying the risk of one of you exposing the S.P.M.A.

Every lesson is about testing your ability as well as your resolve, pushing to see who breaks and who's likely to squeal. *That's* why things are changing now; the time for innocent wonder is over. If you really want to be part of our world, you need to understand *all* aspects of it: light and dark. This isn't fairytale living."

With the black dust filtering through the holes in the walls, stretching towards The Cendryll skylight, the class studied their teacher, standing in his typical casual attire: jeans, untucked shirt, jumper and Society tie.

They admired Jacob for his exploits in war, frequently stunned by his magical powers. Trust had never been an issue and wasn't now, but *fear* was a new visitor to the group. After all, lessons had focused on gentle topics like healing remedies, cool artefacts and the geography of the S.P.M.A.

Their makeshift, fifth-floor classroom became the only place they wanted to be, concocting potions and practising creative charms — lessons that burst with showers of light and delighted laughter as one miracle after another formed. There was *nothing* like the S.P.M.A. they knew, reminding themselves that their final trials weren't too far away: when they would fall or fly.

Protecting themselves from vampiric birds was the taste of things to come, they realised, returning to their desks as their steel frames snapped back into smaller shapes — candles, pens, ornaments and magnifying glasses — all resting on their desks as the morning's lesson continued. The Quij remained stationed on the edge of their desks, their wings fluttering and bodies glowing.

"Well, that wasn't a bad start," Jacob uttered, offering his class a warm smile, "so maybe it's time to learn how to attack."

"Yes!" came the collective shouts of the class, forgetting their fears at the offer of new, magical powers.

"Rucklz has clearly improved your reflexes, suggesting we can move onto counterfire: the best remedy of all."

"So, we're going to kill the vampiric birds this time?" Leah Creswell asked, smiling as she always did.

"No, Leah, we're going to try to touch the sky."

"Flying?" the tiny figure of Olin Zucklewick queried.

"Striking," Jacob offered with a smile, adding, "With fire and ice."

"Here?" queried Tom, watching as the bottle-blue Quij rested on his arm.

"Out there," their teacher replied, pointing behind him.

"Above ground?"

"No, on top of the world."

A reply which left the group stumped, watching as streaks of light appeared from Jacob's steel cane, creating a portable Perium. "It's time to feel the true force of magic."

With that, they were off, stepping through a circle of light into an unfamiliar space where new adventures lay.

THE SPACE THEY ENTERED WAS NOTHING LIKE THE CRAMPED, fifth-floor quarters they used for a classroom. This room had twisted walls and no ceiling to speak of. The walls reminded Ethan and Tom of staircases, stretching towards another neverland. The wooden floor was decorated with lines of gold ... lines that shifted each time the students moved.

It was a training chamber of some sort, maybe designed

just for them: apprentices with ambitions of sorcery. Ava and Katie studied the gold-lined floor, moving their feet to work out its function, but the secrets remained in the chamber for now.

As Jacob stepped into the centre of the room, uttering Exhibius, a shaft of light appeared from high above, streaming down onto the classmates and their teacher. With the light flooding the space, the lessons continued.

"Before we head out into proper daylight," Jacob stated, "I wanted to bring you here to Heaven's Chamber. We've got an afternoon of fun lined up later, testing your speed of thought in a game of Rucklz. However, before we do that, I want you to learn about two powerful elements: fire and ice. Both charms can be used to protect and destroy although protection is always the aim.

"Can you reach the top?" Tilly asked, her freckled face looking less sullen.

"If you're lucky," Jacob replied, clapping for the class to stand in line with him.

With the group standing together, four on each side of their young teacher, Jacob explained the principles of Heaven's Chamber.

'The gold lines you see on the floor are pathways: eight pathways for eight students. Use your penchants to touch the floor. When you do, your penchant stones will begin to glow and the gold lines will run along the floor, towards the walls."

"The walls look like staircases," Olin commented, shaking his brown fringe away from his eyes.

"They are in a way," Jacob replied, lifting his cane towards the wooden walls. "Staircases or race tracks; however you want to view it."

"And they take us to the sky?" Ava asked, cracking her

knuckles in preparation for another test.

"Depending on how successful you are."

"And if we're not, we use the flight charm as we fall?"

"No flight charm," Jacob explained. "Another protective blanket will be in place if you fall."

"What charm's that?" Ethan asked, patting his afro in a sign of nervous anticipation.

"The Fora charm: an invisible barrier halting the momentum of falling objects. That's my job. Your job is to get ready to race to the sky."

That was enough to get the group buzzing with excitement, chatting amongst themselves until Jacob threw his cane in the air, catching the silver whistle in his hand: the magic of morphing steel.

"We learn the fire charm first, then ice magic if that goes to plan. The aim of the game is to generate fire as you race along your gold lines. If you stray off your line, you'll fall. If you're knocked off your line, you'll fall. If you fail to produce fire, I'll send ice your way to signal you're out of the game."

"What's the aim of the game?" Katie asked, ever the competitive spirit.

The general dress code of the students was jeans, T-shirts and jumpers although Katie rarely wore anything but jeans and T-shirts, even when it was blisteringly cold outside. Her fierce competitiveness had backfired on her so far, often losing out to the skill and wit of whoever was on Olin's team: the boy with a gift for magical living.

"The aim of the game is to not come last," Jacob said, raising his palms upwards as he did. He looked every bit the teacher, the Society tie hanging loosely over his shirt as he whispered the charm to release fire: "*Infernisi.*"

The classmates took cover as streaks of fire flooded upwards, powerful energy pouring from Jacob's upturned hands as he looked on. The stunned look on the students' faces said it all — this was *way* more advanced than they'd expected, having only just learnt creative charms.

There was no time to waste though, making Ethan wonder what else had caused this sudden sense of urgency in the Society elders. Maybe a student from another faculty had already messed up, having their mind altered as they were sent back to above-ground living.

Maybe the legendary Casper and Philomeena Renn had expressed doubts, marking out some of the class for failure. Whatever it was, their young teacher was more intense, giving no time to his usual anecdotes and war stories. Something was brewing in the S.P.M.A. and Ethan was keen to learn more. First, though, he had to pass this test to not fall into the category of 'concern' — the one place none of the class wanted to be.

"Your lessons in defensive charms have begun," Jacob commented, directing the flood of fire towards the shifting walls on either side. "It's unlikely you'll need them, but complacency is the pastime of fools. On my instruction, close your eyes and clear your minds: things are about to heat up."

Tilly smiled at this joke, the red-headed girl with a superiority complex. Normally, such humour would get a dismissive look, but the sheer *power* of magic on display was enough to humble her. If Tilly wanted to make the grade, a large dose of humility was going to be needed.

She'd heard the stories of Jacob's ability to communicate with Society creatures — how he'd stopped a white Williynx ripping an errant boy-wizard to pieces. The Williynx were the creatures she was most interested in: the beautiful, colourful majestic birds that could shape shift and breath ice.

She remembered how Jacob's sister, Guppy, had appeared in the sky on the back of a power-blue Williynx, the legendary Fire Witch coming to pay her a visit. Guppy was a Night Ranger now, gliding through the Society Sphere with Conrad: a magical couple with war wounds and a gift for sniffing out danger.

Night Ranging sounded like it was up Tilly's street, if she decided magical living was for her. Her sullenness was related to a hidden resentment, linked her parents pressing her to join the experiment. Above-ground living hadn't been so bad, Tilly mused, although a mercurial existence was obviously better.

She just wanted to make sure it was for her, before she committed her life to it. If things didn't work out, there was always the 'Removilis' charm to wipe her memory. A groan of frustration re-focused Tilly as sparks of fire spluttered from Roan's hands, an attempt at magic not improved by a little temper tantrum.

"I *can't do it*," Roan shouted, the relative of a legendary wizard named Aarav Khan: a sky soldier who oversaw the magical realm of Zilom.

"It takes time," Jacob said, placing the silver whistle in his mouth to signal the race to the skies was about to begin. "It helps to trigger rage, so think of something that gets you angry ... *really* angry."

Olin had no problem doing this, touching the wooden floor with his right hand as fire circled around his hands. As he did, the penchant stone in his ring glowed, causing the gold line under his feet to stretch ahead, reaching the wall. The moment it did, Olin shot forward, racing along the floor and up the wall as he spun a lasso of fire above his head: an early advantage for the smallest member of the class.

"*Come on!*" Katie urged with increasing frustration, her

anger rising at the sight of Olin riding the strange stairway on the never-ending wooden walls.

"Think of *beginnings* not endings," Jacob said, taking the whistle out of his mouth.

With Ethan, Leah and Roan shooting off with fire blasting from their hands, only Katie, Tilly and Tom were left: three apprentices who were battling doubt. Tom carried the weight of a relative's sin, while Katie and Tilly were sinking in a combination of sarcasm and insecurity. Doubt had never helped witches or wizards in battle and it wasn't going to help them now, leaving Jacob to lend a helping hand.

"*Beginnings* not endings," Jacob said again. "Think of a point when you felt powerless. Hold onto that rage and channel it through your body. Critically, don't let go of the feeling when sparks of fire form. Clear your mind and return to a moment that sparks rage. You have thirty seconds before I blow the whistle, then you're out of the game."

The three classmates knew what that meant — a mark against their name and doubts regarding their ability. Too many failures led to expulsion so it was time to get angry, returning to a beginning triggering uncomfortable memories. Whatever they chose, the trick worked in seconds, generating lines of fire streaking upwards like searchlights investigating the mysteries of an endless space.

Katie, Tilly and Tom had ground to make up but they also had an advantage, watching how the lines arced and twisted on the strange, shifting walls ... lines that ran straight like a one hundred metre race before intersecting ... causing contact to be made. It was all part of the game, managing fire whilst manoeuvring your way out of danger, seeing who could survive and touch the sky.

3

TOUCHING THE SKY

With the game in full swing, Jacob studied the race to the sky, smiling at the sight of his young students battling to forge ahead as the swirling walls tilted them one way then the other. Additionally, the gold lines that zipped them upwards made the race more interesting, the lines forming a race track as competitive shouts filled the wooden chamber providing this morning's test.

Olin was still ahead, his small frame bending as his gold line arced to the left suddenly, sending him crashing into Ava who managed to spin into the air, landing perfectly on the spiral of light that guided her on.

"Good move!" Jacob shouted encouragingly, ready to activate the blanket of protection.

Fire hadn't come into play yet but it would, particularly when the students realised it helped with acceleration. Leah was the first to work this out, squealing in joy as she sent a fire ball ahead of her, blasting forwards to get level with Olin who was caught off guard momentarily, which is when the race *really* began.

With staircases climbing out of the walls, the strange design of the training chamber became evident — the wooden structure was a stairway to heaven and the last one there would come tumbling to the ground, marked down for a lack of initiative and competitive edge.

"YES!" Roan shouted as he somersaulted onto the nearest stairway, sending streaks of fire ahead as the competition heated up, each member of the class finding different ways of using fire to their advantage.

Tilly, Katie and Tom had decided spinning rings of flames were the best way to gain velocity, while Ava, Olin and Roan chose to add fire to their golden lines, judging this to be the most effective method.

Ethan and Leah had found the most effective way, though, sending strings of fire towards the sky as they navigated the colossal staircases bursting into life ... structures with too many steps to count ... acting as an additional hurdle in the race to the top.

Tom was the first victim in the game, sent flying as a staircase burst into life beneath him, his fire charm deactivating the moment he panicked as he fell through the air at frightening speed.

"Fora," Jacob whispered, using the silver cane to send a force field across the space: a shimmering film of light representing the safety net some would need.

Tom's tumbling figure halted inches away from the blanket of protection ... his thin, pale frame hanging upside down as competitive shouts and blasts of fire filled the air. The embarrassment was evident on his face, the quiet boy battling with the ghost of an infamous relative.

"Go again," Jacob encouraged. "The race isn't over yet."

"I'm out," Tom said, looking down at the teacher who gave him the chance of a lifetime. "I knew it would be me."

"Self-pity is your worst enemy, Tom. You're going to be a brilliant wizard so shake it off and *go again*."

"How?" Tom asked, his black hair sticking up as if he'd had an electric shock.

"The true power is in the sky," Jacob explained, uttering "Spintz" as a shower of light floated upwards. "Target your fire at the pinnacle of this tower and hold on."

"Like a rocket launch?" Tom asked, excited at the idea of a spectacular second chance.

"Exactly like a rocket launch. Prepare your fire before it's too late."

Stepping back, Jacob watched as Tom grew in confidence, shaking off a temporary failure. Raising his right arm to the sky, he remembered Jacob's advice regarding beginnings not endings, clearing your mind before returning to a memory that triggered rage. That was easy for Tom, his memory returning to an uncle that had stained the family name for eternity: Erent Koll.

"Infernisi!" Tom shouted, watching in astonishment as a charge of fire blasted upwards, surging through his thin frame before he shot into the air like a rocket, learning to bend the line of fire to avoid the crashing staircases that continued to blast out of the walls.

Suddenly, he was more confident, like a gymnast executing every move to perfection. With Olin and Leah still in front, charging up staircases leading to the sky, Tom used a different method to gain ground, jumping off each staircase that burst into view, using them as platforms to launch himself forward.

It was a perfect plan, the rocket fuel of fire sending him on a spectacular trajectory as he discovered an agility, bending and twisting to avoid fragments of wood that flew in every direction as the walls exploded, leaving only a maze of steps climbing in their own race to heaven.

"Brilliant," Jacob whispered, throwing the silver whistle into the air and catching a mug. Uttering 'Comeuppance' to retrieve a vial of white liquid from his pocket, he poured the remedy into the mug, taking a sip. He still didn't know what the remedy was called or what it did, but it beat Liqin when you needed total focus.

Kerevenn, the ageing giant, had used the white remedy to heal his sister's wounds. Jacob knew why it was needed — understanding injuries sustained in the sky realms were beyond normal Society remedies— but wondered why the secret had been kept about the properties of the mysterious concoction. For now, he was happy to sip it, inhaling its sweet smell: a permanent reminder of a sister he loved and missed.

As the race neared its close with Ethan and Katie overtaking Olin, Jacob readied himself for his own take off, deciding a flight charm would be sufficient until the jaws of broken staircases posed a problem. He would then use a doorway of light to vanish through, happy in the knowledge he'd passed all Society tests, no longer needing to prove his worth.

"Propellus Celiri," Jacob uttered, holding his silver mug in one hand as a daisy wrapped itself around his left hand, the flower rotating like a propellor as he was lifted off the ground.

Magical living was spectacular all right, and he had no intention of ever returning to the above-ground world. There were too many memories and too many friends now, some still with him and some perished.

Loss hadn't changed his perception of the S.P.M.A. any more than war had. In the end, it was a simple choice between mundane living or magical mayhem. For Jacob, there would only ever be one winner.

With Ethan shouting in victory at the pinnacle of Heaven's Chamber, Jacob made his appearance, darting through a portal of light to the surprise of those who'd made it to the top. Roan and Ava had fallen at the last hurdle, knocked off their lines of gold by the jagged edges of splintering stairways.

Their frustrated yells could be heard as they tumbled through the air, activating Velinis charms to avoid being burnt by clouds of fire. Safely tucked within their protective bubbles of protection — tinged in the colour of their penchant stones — Roan and Ava remembered the rule of no flight charms if they failed, trusting their teacher had created the safety net he'd promised.

After all, *dead* students weren't part of the training. Ava's scream suggested she feared the worst, desperately trying to activate the flight charm as the wooden floor got closer, only for the two of them to freeze in mid-flight, arms and legs spread as the power of the force field was felt ... a blanket of protection they sat on as the training continued above them.

"Damn it!" Ava shouted, her tall, athletic body letting her down for once. Rubbing her head in frustration, she punched at the barrier of light holding her and Roan up, staring up at the sliver of light in anger.

It seemed an impossible distance from where they were sitting, but magic had negotiated the space. Now, though, they wouldn't be part of any critical learning going on, knowing every missed opportunity was a gap in their knowledge, and one that might come back to haunt them.

"*Say something,*" Ava demanded, elbowing the student she was closest to.

"We didn't make it," Roan said with a shrug of the shoulders, the most philosophical of the group. The Khan name was synonymous with magical majesty, he knew, but also with tragedy. Loss was part of the game and part of life in general. It was arrogant and petulant to think life always worked out in your favour: it didn't.

"And now we don't know what's going on *up there,*" Ava continued, shuffling closer to the friend whose calm nature she was drawn to.

The other girls questioned her about her feelings for Roan, but she dismissed their interest. It was friendship plain and simple, Ava uncertain of matters of the heart.

"We'll find out," Roan replied, the two of them remaining in their bubbles of protection. Splinters of wood continued to rain down, suggesting deactivating the Velinis charm would be a bad idea. "You should put some Srynx Serum on that," Roan added, gesturing towards the blood on Ava's ankles.

"Those *bloody staircases*," Ava said before taking Roan's advice, uttering 'Comeuppance' as she reached for a vial of orange liquid: the remedy to heal wounds.

"Where did you get cut?"

"On my waist but it's basically a scratch."

"Do you think Ethan will tell us when they get back?"

"He'll tell us or Leah will."

"Then we can practice whatever they've learnt up there together."

"Yep," Roan replied with a smile. "Later tonight when they're all asleep."

"Sounds romantic," Ava joked, rubbing the Srynx Serum into her wounds.

"I try to please," Roan joked, happy for a reprieve from the sudden intensity.

"We can stuff ourselves full of sweets and practice new spells."

"It's a date," Roan replied, offering his friend a smile as a cracking sound filled the space before their classmates reappeared, yelling in alarm as blasts of ice fired towards them, courtesy of colourful, shape-shifting birds brought in to conclude the assessment.

"*Wow*," Ava commented. "Williynx *firing* on us?"

"Jacob did say things were going to heat up."

"Someone's going to get killed."

"It's all part of the training," Roan added, assuring his friend. "Look, the Williynx aren't firing directly at them — their ice blasts halt inches before they make contact. It's another test of our skill and dexterity, probably linked to the Rucklz game later."

"Do you think we'll be playing Rucklz on the back of Williynx?"

"Now, that *would* be amazing considering we've never flown one."

"No time like the present," Ava added, standing in her bubble of protection to watch the spectacle ... Leah, Tom and Ethan struggling to follow the gold lines back down as the staircases retreated into the shifting walls, having played their part in the morning's assessment. Katie, Olin and Tilly were fairing a little better, looking like they'd worked out the Williynx attack was false fire.

"*Brilliant*," Ava commented as a shower of feathers was released from the majestic creatures ... blue, yellow, red, pink and white ... as if a ceremony was coming to an end which in a way it was ... a ceremony marking the beginning of dangerous living.

"Not bad for your first attempt," Jacob said, gliding back down on a carpet of feathers like a king.

"What was up there?" Ava asked Leah who offered her a wink.

"Later," Leah whispered, the class focused on the Williynx as they touched down, all hoping for the news that flight was part of today's wizardry.

"Obviously, our feathered friends would never do a Society member harm," Jacob added, sipping from his silver mug, "unless they've asked for it."

"Like Taeia Renn," Olin uttered, realising this wasn't a topic Jacob was willing to discuss.

"What's up there?" Roan asked, deciding to change the subject.

"Everything and nothing," Jacob replied with a smile. "Anyway, time to learn to mount a Williynx before our game of Rucklz later."

"*YESSSSS!*" came the collective cry of joy from eight students immersed in the adventure of a lifetime.

4
SPARKS OF SORCERY

With the morning assessment over, the class made their way to the place where the game of Rucklz would take place: The Hallowed Lawn. The name came from the fact that dead legends were buried there — Society soldiers who had given their life in battle. Rumour had it that the ashes of the dead rose from the ground when a witch or wizard was in need, but none of students had ever witnessed such a thing.

Mystery was entwined with magic in the S.P.M.A., and the mystery of how you vanished out of sight was on today's agenda. Jacob had mentioned the art of vanishing on entering the classroom this morning, stepping through a portal to break up the students' magical antics.

The class knew all about the Disira charm, but also knew it was prohibited unless absolutely necessary. To some degree, it was an unstable charm due to the reliance on a clear mind. You had to picture your destination before activating the charm, the danger laying in having an unclear location in mind. When that happened, you ended up in dangerous realms where feral creatures and vampire birds lay in wait.

After experiencing the Ameedis earlier — screeching out of Jacob's Zombul in a blizzard of black menace — the students were crystal clear on the dangers of the vanishing charm. Now, it was time to put their understanding to the test: a game of Rucklz where vanishing acts were part of the assessment.

With The Hallowed Lawn decorated by the presence of colourful, majestic Williynx, Jacob ushered the class nearer as the wind lifted. "Before the game of Rucklz begins, we need to practice the art of vanishing as promised. There are two rules which *everyone* must stick to."

Glancing at Ethan and Katie as he said this, Jacob continued. "Rule number one: you can only vanish to a *known* place that is *safe* and familiar. Rule number two: if you end up in no-man's-land, activate protective charms and *wait for help*. Anyone breaking these rules will be expelled."

A murmur of unease ran through the group at this news: expulsion for any critical errors. It made Ethan wonder again if someone *had* already been expelled, making him even more determined to get his hands on a Follygrin: a small, circular notebook that helped you locate the whereabouts of any Society member.

"Choose your teams and mount your Williynx," Jacob instructed, patting the neck of the fire-red Williynx closest to him. "And remember, *no room for error*."

Jacob watched from the sidelines as the students argued amongst themselves, Ethan and Katie fighting for the best Rucklz players to ensure they had an advantage. As always, it wasn't as simple as brute force — skill and subtlety typically won Rucklz matches, as well as the critical principle of unity.

Ethan and Katie had yet to work out that self-interest wasn't enough, Olin being the leader in this field. The smallest member of the class, Olin had learned to turn an assumed weakness to his advantage, never putting himself forward or forcing the issue but, instead, observing the dynamics of the group to know where and when to engage.

After a few minutes of debate and an impatient clap from Jacob, the teams were chosen and Williynx were mounted — the tradition of learning to engage the majestic creatures carried out. All living things in the Society had equal status, meaning creatures needed to be treated with the uppermost respect.

After all, Williynx could splinter a person into a thousand pieces with a blast of ice, not something any of the classmates wanted to experience.

"Take your positions!" Jacob shouted as each Williynx released a feather as they took off from the ground, carrying their young companions into the air.

As each coloured feather touched the ground, a line of light appeared, running along the perimeter of The Hallowed Lawn to mark the boundary of the pitch. More feathers fell to create the dots throughout the pitch ... dots which determined the rules of the game.

The rules of Rucklz were simple. Each player had to activate a dot to enter the game. Once the dot was activated, the player had to imagine the most appropriate shape to attack or defend with. The aim of the game was to strike out your opponents until no players were left on the opposing side.

Originally a board game, the Society elders had decided Rucklz was a perfect game to train students. After all, it simulated battle without the possibility of fatal injury, which wasn't to say there was no danger involved.

One false move could splinter bones and rip through

flesh although this wasn't the aim of today's game. To survive the game and the assessment, vanishing had to be mastered which is where the Disira charm came in.

"We practice disappearing before the game begins!" Jacob shouted from the perimeter of the pitch. "Think of *one* location to vanish to and *stick* to this place. When you find yourself in danger in the game, disappear to this place and *reappear* within *ten seconds*. That's the focus of this assessment."

"*Ten seconds?*" Tilly queried, her red hair flowing in the wind as her yellow Williynx hovered above The Hallowed Lawn.

"Not a second more," Jacob added. "If you're going to live in this world, you need speed and dexterity because things have a habit of *occurring* in the S.P.M.A."

"Like another war?" Ethan asked, grimacing when his fire-red Williynx released a mild roar.

"Like mastering the art of secrecy, Ethan," Jacob replied. "The biggest concern the Society elders have. Children are notorious for having loose tongues. Loose tongues in a secret Society leads to devastation. The Disira charm allows you to move like a ghost when necessary, making sure you leave no trace of Society business above ground.

Of course, *how* you vanish is critical because any suspicion of supernatural activity will draw unwanted attention."

"Can we start now?" Roan asked, adjusting his stick-thin frame on the back of his turquoise Williynx.

"On my whistle," Jacob replied, raising an arm to build anticipation in the group.

With the two teams facing off against each other — Tilly, Ava, Tom and Ethan vs Leah, Katie, Olin and Roan — the whistle was blown and the action began ... each student darting down on their feathered companions to touch a glimmering dot with their fingers ... rising up again to form the object required to engage in a test of skill and wit.

ETHAN'S TEAM MOVED IN FORMATION, TOUCHING THEIR DOTS and rising high into the sky, out of range of the spears of light Roan and Leah let fly. Added to this was the speed and shape-shifting ability of the Williynx, the majestic creatures swerving out of harm's way with ease as Ethan hatched the plan.

. "I say we storm down towards them, releasing ball bearings as we do. Hundreds of ball bearings to break their formation then we vanish to our safe places, returning in ten seconds behind them."

Tilly, Ava and Tom nodded, used to following the orders of the boy with the Lyell family name: Lyell being synonymous with leadership in the S.P.M.A. They'd been promised a visit from Weyen Lyell, the Caribbean legend from The Orium Circle: the faculty that made all magical laws.

Ava hoped Weyen Lyell would appear at their graduation, shaking their hands to formally welcome them to The Society for the Preservation of Magical Artefacts. That was assuming she *did* graduate which wasn't a given.

She wasn't one of the children with a famous family name, making her wonder how gifted she was, but she had the determination to make up for any magical misgivings.

"Ready when you are," she replied to Ethan, enjoying the feeling of the wind rushing through her brown hair as they descended as one ... a combined force dodging spears of light as they closed in on the opposition ... releasing their dots of light into the weapon of choice ... a rain of ball bearings storming towards the target.

"Move!" Katie shouted at the sight of the counterattack, secretly fearing a blast of Williynx ice would follow it. "Vanishing positions," she added but Olin was ahead of the game, pressing his face into his feathered companion as he vanished out of sight.

Roan and Leah were slower to react, managing to vanish as the shower of ball bearings struck home, smashing into their arms and shoulders as the Williynx transported them out of danger.

"Not bad," came a familiar voice behind Jacob: Casper Renn.

The elegant leader of The Cendryll appeared from a portal of light, stepping through the glimmering purple circle in an immaculate, light-blue suit.

"Morning, Casper," Jacob offered with a smile, shaking the scarred hand of a Society legend.

"Any concerns?" Casper asked, joining Jacob on the perimeter of the Rucklz pitch, resting in silence before an explosive return to battle.

"Just a bit of arrogance to contain."

"Ethan and Katie?"

"And Tilly to a degree, although I think Tilly's centres around a lack of confidence. Are they all sticking to the curfew?"

"Not all," Casper replied, taking a blue handkerchief from his pocket to dab at his eye, "but we're keeping an eye on things. They won't all make it, Jacob, and the ones that do will have a lot to learn on the way."

"Do you think the Society elders regret the idea?"

"We made a promise to respect the principle of unity. Whether it was the right decision remains to be seen."

As these words were exchanged, the two teams reappeared but not in their previous formations, Tilly struggling to keep her balance as her Williynx whipped her out of danger, whilst Tom offered additional protection to his teammate, activating a secondary vanishing charm with the utterance of 'Verum Veras'.

"Looks like she's had a shock," Casper commented as Tilly's fire-red Williynx climbed higher until she and Tom faded behind a curtain of protection.

"If she goes too high, she'll fall," Jacob said as a look of concern crossed his face.

"They have to fall or fly, Jacob, like you did."

"It's harder on this side of the fence, teaching rather than experiencing."

"But it gives you an insight into a future generation," Casper replied, dabbing at his eyes again. "A generation we'll come to rely on more and more as time passes, and old comrades pass on. Trust the process, Jacob. After all, magic invariably comes to the rescue of the young."

"Except for one," Jacob countered, turning his attention to Roan who did well to avoid a scythe ripping him to pieces. Roan's brooding character was partly linked to the loss of a relative in the last battle, a friend Jacob still thought of whenever he ventured to The Singing Quarter.

Magic *usually* came to the rescue of the young, but not always, something he knew too well. It needed to come to the rescue of Tilly who reappeared in the sky, gliding back into the mayhem of the Rucklz battle that had sent Leah, Ava and Olin crashing out of the game.

"They will all find their strengths in time," Casper offered as shooting arrows appeared behind a shield of protection, keeping Katie out of harm's way, but Katie didn't have her eyes on the sky as Tilly tumbled off her feathered companion, bringing the game to a standstill.

"Wait," Casper instructed as Jacob stepped onto the

pitch, readying to stop her fall. "Skill cannot be found where safety exists."

That was true enough, Jacob knew, suppressing his concern as he watched Tilly tumble towards The Hallowed Lawn ... the sacred field lit up by multi-coloured light.

"Wait," Casper said again as the students turned to Jacob for help, resting on the back of their Williynx as fear kicked in.

"*Do something!*" Ava shouted from the sidelines, sending a Spintz charm into the air to shower Tilly with light. "*She's there. Do something!*"

But Jacob didn't, knowing Casper Renn's word was final. The man who had seen so much and understood even more ... proof of this evident in the way Tilly spun into life ... her hands touching the ground as she activate a dot to strike out at Katie and Roan ... the surviving members of the opposition who reacted too late.

The golden web they were caught in signalled the end of the Rucklz game and victory for Tilly's team, although the question of what had caused her stricken state had yet to be answered. Each student had vanished and returned within the ten-second limit, but only Tilly had reappeared looking ashen and lifeless, suggesting her vanishing charm had taken her *elsewhere* ...

∼

"What happened?" Tom asked as the rows of dots faded from the Rucklz pitch.

"She won, that's what happened," Katie barked spitefully, glaring at the girl she had a strange hatred for.

"Skill and wit," Casper added, stepping towards the group who fell silent.

No one challenged Casper Renn — the man who was likely to decide on their future in the S.P.M.A. "The art of Rucklz is to gain an edge, after all, and sometimes the most subtle manoeuvres are the best ones."

"So, *what happened?*" Tom asked again, remembering how Tilly had almost fainted as they climbed higher in the sky.

"I ended up in the wrong place," Tilly replied, blinking repeatedly as she sat on the grass, surrounded by classmates expressing concern — except for Katie.

"Where?" Ava asked.

"Quibbs Causeway."

The words drew gasps from the others ... the mention of a deadly passage of land surrounded by water enough to generate more questions.

"Did the Mantzils get to you?" Ethan asked, shocked at the idea of invisible, screeching creatures penetrating Tilly's mind.

"I don't remember," Tilly replied, "except for someone appearing and getting me out in time."

"Who?" Ava asked, just as another familiar face appeared through an archway of light — Philomeena Renn — sister of Casper Renn and second-in-command in The Cendryll.

"Did the trick work?" she asked.

Tilly nodded with a smile: "Perfectly."

"Drink this," Philomeena added, handing Tilly a vial of yellow liquid: Liqin to remedy the senses. "Your assessments are over for the day. The afternoon is yours to do as you please."

"Can we go above ground?" Ethan asked, desperately wanting to taste another milkshake in Merrymopes.

"You can," Philomeena replied, taking something else

out of her red bag, "but be mindful of the consequences of drawing attention to yourselves."

"Memory wiped and no more magic," Ethan added with an excited smile, knowing there was another magical treat in Merrymopes ice cream and milkshake parlour: The Revolving Room.

5
ABOVE GROUND ANTICS

Founders' Quad was its usual bustle of eager shoppers, keen to experience the wonders of Leaning Lane — the strange sight of each building on the famous street getting smaller until you got to Wimples sweet shop, the smallest of them all. Enticing to children and puzzling to adults, Wimples was the place a certain group of young witches and wizards were headed.

Using one of the doors on the ground floor of The Cendryll, four of Jacob's students stepped onto the streets of Founders' Quad via a shop they rarely visited these days: Cribbe & Corrow. One of the quieter establishments in the popular market town of Bibsley Corbett, Cribbe & Corrow was the shop you got your penchant from — the item giving you access to a secret, magical universe.

Having survived the morning's trials, including learning how to disappear as well as flying on the back of a magical creature, it was time for the magicians in training to have some fun.

"Wimples then Merrymopes," Ethan suggested, turning

the ring on the forefinger of his right hand, the item allowing him magical travel.

"Deal," Ava replied, striding alongside her classmates as above-ground crowds jostled to enter popular establishments.

As well as Wimples and Merrymopes, there was Pat's Caff that drew more adults than children — the strange concoctions doing something to the senses. Of course, above-ground customers had no idea of the source of the flavoured drinks — Society remedies giving a lift to those living more mundane lives.

Wimples was a more chaotic affair all together, largely because entering was part of the fun. The smallest building in Founders' Quad posed problems for adults, making it a haven for children who could escape their parents' clutches temporarily ... the sound of children laughing in delight as they reached for the boxes of strangely named wonders: *Codswollops* and *Core Blimeys* to name a few.

The best part of all was the impression left on your tongue, moving illustrations of the figure found on the sweet box. It was a simple touch of Society sorcery, drawing screams of delight from children and befuddlement on the faces of parents. *How* the illustrations moved was in the 'secret recipe', the elderly owners explained: Society folk skilled in the art of operating in plain sight.

Touches of wonder were found throughout Founders' Quad, its name reflecting the origins of the S.P.M.A. Wonder had become the norm for Jacob's students, still in awe of the magical world they'd only scratched the surface of.

They'd been studied for some time by the Society elders, assessments of their character and personality carried out via surveillance devices such as Follygrins. Other children had failed to pass this basic test, too volatile with tongues that wagged at the first opportunity.

Secrecy and integrity were critical elements of Society living, something drilled into The Fateful Eight on entering a world of wonder. One mistake would end their magical adventure: an adventure increasing in intensity day-by-day. Vampiric birds blasting out of a silver artefact got everyone's attention earlier, before Tilly found herself on a mind-bending strip of land: Quibbs Causeway.

It was fair to say they'd earned a break above ground, the students splitting up into two groups of four, reflecting the friendships forging between them.

"Looks like the Society elders are out in force," Roan commented, gesturing towards the familiar faces roaming through Founders' Quad, engaged in conversation whilst keeping an eye on their young apprentices.

Youth had been critical to the Society's survival in recent times, leading to a realisation that much could be learned from the young. Impulsivity was also a feature of the young, bringing with it obvious dangerous of exposure: the reason Society soldiers were out in force whenever the class made an appearance above ground.

The students had yet to understand the extent of the surveillance, every shop run by Society members as well as every street corner. There was surveillance in the skies as well, sky urchins hovering behind a protective film of light, hiding them from above-ground eyes.

With Scribberals rattling and Panorilums floating within Society faculties, nothing the group did went unnoticed.

"It's the Melackin who creep me out," commented Ava. "That'll be our fate if we mess up."

"I doubt the Society adults would go *that far*," Leah countered, her black hair falling over her shoulders.

"They might," Ethan suggested, dressed in brown corduroys and a grey jumper. "If we *really* mess up."

"Well, we'll be scavenging a living if we do," Roan added in a casual manner, waving at the group of ladies who smiled as they passed.

"Always so positive," Ava teased, less demure than the other girls but equal in magical might.

"Just being realistic. They look like secret police, ready to report back on our every move."

"Well, so far we've crossed the road and almost knocked over a pensioner," Leah quipped with a light laugh, the girl who always seemed at ease.

"I messed up in Heaven's Chamber this morning," Roan mused, "meaning there's another mark against my name."

"Me too," Ava added, tying her brown hair into a bob, "so we need to tread carefully above ground: no mishaps or expulsion is a definite."

"We've all failed at different things," Ethan offered reassuringly, "so don't overthink it. There's plenty of time to prove ourselves."

"Or not," Ava replied, adding, "so what was at the top of Heaven's Chamber?"

"The borders of The Society Sphere, I think," Ethan replied. "It felt a bit like heaven standing up there."

"How do you mean?"

"The way the clouds brushed your face," Leah added. "The most I could make out was the outline of mountains and lightning shooting down in the distance — the reason we thought it was the boundaries of The Society Sphere."

"Where things get interesting," Roan added, wishing he'd been able to avoid the staircase blasting from the walls.

"Well, it looks like things are about to get interesting now," Ava added, pointing to a girl who collapsed to her knees outside Wimples sweet shop, holding her throat as her face turned a worrying shade of red ... the scattering children offering cover to the figure who made her way along Leaning Lane.

"What do we do?" Leah queried, the permanent smile fading from her face.

"Help obviously," Ava replied with mild disdain, her tall, angular figure breaking into a run.

"Maybe it's another assessment," Roan added as the classmates rushed towards the girl, slumped to her knees as the choking fit worsened.

"We'd better pass it then," Ethan added, sensing his friend was right — all Society eyes on them as their skill and wit was put to the test once more.

"Ellie!" came the voice of a panicked parent: a mother in her early thirties with a look of terror on her face.

What to do became the immediate concern, Ethan abandoning their afternoon plans to put his mercurial skills to the test. Whatever they did had to appear natural, no sudden activation of charms possible as a crowd of concerned onlookers gathered around.

"Help!" came the mother's shout as the girl turned purple, collapsing to the floor as she did. "Help me!"

Easing through the crowds, Ava took Roan's hand and whispered the plan, hoping she was right about the questionable character who'd vanished from view. With a nod from Roan, the pair edged closer to the girl before they whispered 'Undilum': the spell to deactivate charms.

The hoped for effect was realised as the girl began to cough, gasping for air she could now inhale, leading to a mixture of puzzled faces looking on and the expected conclusions ... choking on her favourite sweet ... caught in a fit of laughter that had almost cost her life ... the girl unable to counter these theories as her mother hugged her tightly, offering the classmates a strange look.

With the panic subsiding, interest returned to shopping as the crowd dispersed, leaving the four classmates to step away before attention turned to them.

"That was close," Roan commented as faces appeared in shop windows, Society folk looking on as a new drama unfolded.

"And weird," Ethan added, frustrated not to have thought of the obvious solution. "Someone trying to choke a kid to death."

"But who?" Leah posed. "Test or no test, we need to find out."

"A pretty cruel way of testing us, if that's what this is," Ava added.

"Only one way to find out," Ethan added, determined to succeed in this next trial. "Find the weirdo who did it."

"Easier said than done," Roan countered, "since we can't pop a Follygrin open to check their whereabouts."

"So we find a place where we can: Merrymopes."

With the afternoon taking a dramatic turn, thoughts of magical sweets and milkshakes were parked. It was time to locate the whereabouts of a witch who'd tried to strangle a young girl with some sort of charm: a witch either working with the S.P.M.A. to continue their trials above ground or with another agenda in mind.

To find her, they needed to access a spinning structure

located beneath Merrymopes ice cream and milkshake parlour — The Revolving Room — and this meant gaining the favour of the famous twins who ran the establishment: Henkle and Beven Merrymope.

"Did you notice how no Society member reacted?" Ava stated as they sat in a red-and-white booth, studying the busy streets. "As if it was planned."

"Choking a kid to get our attention?" Leah queried. "A bit much, don't you think?"

"Who knows? Either way, we need to find out who the woman is."

"We should let the others know," Leah suggested, turning her attention to the brass bell that rang in the private booth of Merrymopes: a sign of their acceptance from twin brothers with exacting standards.

"We can't do that until we're back in The Cendryll," Ava countered, tapping her fingers on the table, hoping they'd have time to squeeze a milkshake in, something telling her they were in for a long afternoon. "We can use a Scribberal to send them a note when we're back."

"Unless they've got their own test to pass," Roan added, catching the attention of the Merrymope brothers who made their way to the private booth, the wooden door whooshing open of its own accord.

"The trials of the young," Henkle and Beven Merrymope stated in unison, nodding as they did. Dressed in red-and-white, the brothers looked good for their advancing ages, tall and slight with an air of mild-mannered menace about them.

"Afternoon," the classmates offered, knowing the consequences of poor manners.

"Afternoon to you all," came the reply as the brass bell rang again. "It seems you've stumbled upon a problem."

"The choking girl?" Ethan asked.

"Indeed ... the choking girl and the mystery woman causing the scene."

"Do you know her?"

"An erratic witch with a habit of overreacting."

"So, choking the girl was a mistake?" Ava queried, tapping her feet as the exhilaration rushed through her.

"Not quite," the twins replied in unison as the crowds passed by the window, "although it gives you an opportunity to gain ground. After all, we can't all get to heaven at the first attempt."

Roan and Ava exchanged a glance, aware this comment was directed at them. They'd failed to ascend Heaven's Chamber earlier in the day, caught off guard by staircases blasting from the walls of the training space. The twins' reference implied synchronicity extended beyond their famous establishment, a seemingly random attack looking more like an opportunity to prove their worth.

"So, the girl wasn't really in danger?" Ava prompted.

"Not with Society forces on every corner," came the explanation, a synchronised sweep of arms signalling the mingling of magical and non-magical crowds. "You responded appropriately, however, the very thing expected of any Society solider. The only question remaining is what to do now ..."

"What do you mean?" Roan asked, desperate to devour a Belly Blitz, the milkshake that made the Society establishment famous throughout the land.

"Should you leave a loose end or tie it up?" the twins posed, raising their eyebrows as they did. "We've explained the witch in question is erratic, but nothing else. Is this enough for you? Can you rest with this uncertainty?"

"But, you said the girl wasn't in danger?" Ava stated.

"Correct, Miss Blin."

"So, we don't need to do anything."

"Unless our mysterious comrade strikes again ... in the middle of the night perhaps ... another child's screams ringing through Founders' Quad."

"So, we need to finish the job," Leah stated, understanding the point. "Treat it like a test."

"That is entirely your choice," the twins responded in unison, lifting their red-and-white aprons to place four napkins on the table. "However, before you make your decision, enjoy the treats on offer."

With that, the brass bell rang again and an array of ice creams and milkshakes appeared from the strangest location ... a tray floating down from the wood-panelled ceiling that separated above them ... decorated in red-and-white, of course.

As the tray of wonders rested on their table, thoughts of tracking an unstable witch were parked as a different competition began, the four classmates grappling for the favoured treats in a magical establishment offering time for reflection and refreshments.

"So, do we track her down or not?" Ethan posed, scooping out the remaining dollops of ice cream.

"If we don't and it *is* a test, we lose ground on the others," Ava replied, "so I say yes."

"Me too," Roan added, sensing he should grab every opportunity. He hadn't had the best start, partly due to a niggling fear of where magical living could lead: to dark places and brutal ends.

"Where do you think the others are?" Ethan asked through a mouthful of ice cream, knowing Ava and Roan were right. They were all struggling to make the grade at the moment — Olin and Tilly streets ahead of everyone else.

"Having more fun than us, probably," Leah replied, slurping her multi-coloured milkshake, "unless Tilly's still recovering from her trip to Quibbs Causeway. "

"Just goes to show how dangerous things can get," Ethan commented, wondering how he'd deal with finding himself in no-man's-land: realms laced with monsters and menace.

"You can always head back to your bedroom," Ava replied sarcastically. "You know, leave the dangerous stuff to us. I need to close the gap on the others, but feel free to sit this one out."

"As if," Ethan replied with a cold look. "I made it to the top of Heaven's Chamber, remember. *I'm* not the one with something to prove."

"*Okay*," Leah interjected, getting bored with the debate and delay. "Let's focus on the task at hand. What happened earlier was obviously staged, meaning it's another chance for us to prove ourselves. There's a whole Society watching our every move so let's make a statement. Come on, we've got a crazy witch to find."

6

TONIC FOR TROUBLE

With bellyfuls of milkshake and ice cream, the classmates left Merrymopes on the track of a witch with a bad temper. *Who* she was didn't really matter, Ava thought, sensing this *was* another test they would have to perform well in. After all, how secretive could a Society be if it used magic in broad daylight?

There was no logical explanation for the girl gasping for breath, the bemused crowd dispersing once the crisis was over. No doubt, the girl's mother was happy the inexplicable event had passed, but that didn't mean above-ground people wouldn't talk.

Rumours came and went though, and when evidence was scant any thoughts of supernatural phenomena were dismissed: the reason the S.P.M.A. had existed in plain sight for so long. Every witch and wizard was skilled in the art of subtle sorcery, something the students would have to master if they wanted a future of mercurial wonder.

The Revolving Room, hidden beneath Merrymopes, wasn't required after all, the person of interest moving through the streets of Founders' Quad.

"I say we split up," Ethan suggested, rubbing his hands in anticipation of a new drama.

"I'll go with Ava," Roan replied, preferring the company of a friend over the competitive energy of Ethan Lyell. a boy hoping to reach the heights his grandfather had.

"Okay. I'll stick with Leah. We'll meet back here when we've found out more."

Here was a place known as Blindman's Point, situated to the west of Founders' Quad. Blindman's Point was the designated meeting point above ground, partly because it was close to Wimples and Merrymopes, but also because it was near the western boundary of Society Square.

The students were banned from venturing beyond Society Square, but that didn't stop them wondering what lay beyond. They'd all heard the stories of monsters and mountains and mighty battles, hoping Jacob would tell his war stories one day. For now, though, they had a story of their own to unravel — the mystery of a choking spell cast in broad daylight.

"Where to first?" Roan asked as he and Ava headed out of Blindman's Point.

"The Blind Horseman," Ava replied, sensing the witch in question wasn't hiding at all, but waiting.

"Why there?"

"No idea, but we've got to start somewhere," Ava replied, wondering how quickly she could learn the choking charm used on the girl. After all, you never knew when danger was going to enter from the wings.

THE BLIND HORSEMEN HAD ALL THE SIGNS OF A TYPICAL ALE house, including the line of pumps on the wooden counter, offering the most frequently requested beverages. The upper floor of the establishment was marked as 'Staff Only'. Access was gained via the 'Entrinias' charm: a spell providing access to secret Society spaces.

The plan was simple — to locate the witch who'd cast a choking spell on a girl in broad daylight. In some ways, there'd been no risk to using magic in this situation, mainly because there was no visible sign of sorcery at work. Still, it was *very* unusual and *highly* irregular, expulsion the common consequence of such an act.

Ava and Roan sensed something else was at work, though, particularly since the Merrymope twins didn't seem concerned. Eccentric in their habits and brilliant in their recipes for delicious treats, Henkle and Beven Merrymope were two Society adults in the know, probably placed in a perfect position to oversee the trials of eight young students.

As Ava and Roan made their way to the second floor, passing above-ground adults who eyed them with suspicion, the usual action was carried out when the staircase was free of passing traffic. They entered through the 'Staff Only' door and into separate toilet cubicles, not wanting to draw unwanted attention to themselves.

Once inside, a hand was placed on the wood-panelled wall, followed by an utterance of 'Entrinius' ... a spell that made the wooden panels fold into one another, revealing the secret chamber reserved for Society folk.

"Catch any sight of her?" Roan asked as they sat at the only empty booth, a few regulars gesturing a friendly welcome.

It was accepted practice to have under age magicians in the S.P.M.A. now — an acceptance of the part youth had played in its survival.

"Nope," Ava replied, stretching her long legs under the table.

Often mistaken for a couple, the classmates were firm friends but nothing more. Ava was more concerned with securing a future in the S.P.M.A., having little time for romance as their apprenticeship increased in intensity.

"We'll find her between us," Roan added, catching the attention of the barman.

With two glasses of green liquid placed on the table, the friends were left to ponder the whereabouts of the others, sensing their trials would involve more trips to hidden spaces, some known and some yet to be discovered.

"Did you get a look at her?" Ava asked.

With a shake of his head, Roan added, "Just the grey cloak and black boots, and she had grey hair."

"Not much to go on. We could use a Follygrin if we knew her name."

"Another part of the mystery," Ava said, sipping the Jysyn Juice as she studied that space lined with tables, the S.P.M.A. logo decorating the centre of each.

"I thought it might be the evening witch for a second," Roan continued, "but she's locked up in The Velynx."

"Alice Aradel," Ava uttered, remembering the story Jacob had told them ... of an evening witch in charge of a group of captors ... plying her trade at night. Aradel had crossed the line when she'd targeted Jacob's sister, the legendary Guppy Grayling, leading to a life housed in a building blistered by evil.

The Velynx was another story *altogether*: the faculty housing bad things and bad people. On her most insecure days, Ava worried about ending up *there* after somehow getting tangled up with the wrong people. *How* that could happen was beyond reason, but magic had a way of bending things out of time, including the moral compass of certain witches and wizards.

"Well, I say we drink up and go back to our search," Roan proposed. "Just in case identifying her is part of an assessment."

"Agreed," Ava replied. "Let's use a Follygrin to find out where the others are first. Just in case the woman's about to strangle other kids minding their own business."

With a nod, Roan uttered 'Comeuppance', taking out a circular-bound leather notebook. Opening the brass clasp, he rubbed the letter A until the ink bled into five words: *Ask and you Will Find*. Naming each of their classmates, the friends watched as Ethan and Leah appeared first, standing in the trading lane of Tallis & Crake — the place where Society folk traded magical artefacts.

"No joy there," Ava commented, leaning in to inspect the moving illustration.

"Tilly Flint," Roan added, watching the pages flick to the letter 'T' before Tilly appeared with Tom, wandering up Horsel Hill towards an infamous building.

"I doubt she's hiding out in The Sylent," Ava commented, knowing the history of the building well, "and kids are banned from entering the building anyway."

"Maybe Tilly and Tom just wandering, unaware of what's happened."

"Maybe, but I've got a feeling the woman's nearby."

"The question is where?"

"*There*?" Ava replied, pointing to the figure appearing by the trees lining Horsel Hill, closing in on Tilly and Tom who seemed none the wiser. "Let's go."

A portable Perium was the fastest mode of transport, Ava deciding to enact invisibility charms as they stepped through a glimmering archway of light. After all, they couldn't just appear on top of the hill, popping into existence in full view of onlookers.

That would *definitively* get them kicked out. Instead, a protective curtain would mask them from prying eyes, including the woman with more choking charms in mind.

"We need to get to Tilly and Tom before she pulls another stunt," Ava said as they grabbed onto ropes of light illuminating the darkness within, each Cympgus (the name for portable Periums) having its own magical design.

"That's going to be tricky," Roan stated as they prepared to reappear, ensuring their blanket of invisibility was intact, "because she's closing in on them."

"A way of getting their attention then."

"Like what?"

"Like this," Ava replied, whispering 'Spintz' to send a tiny streak of light towards her classmates ... a light so fine no onlookers could distinguish its source ... floating through the air towards Tilly and Tom until it caught their attention.

"What now?" Roan asked, sensing the mysterious woman had more tricks up her sleeve.

"Avoid a choking curse for starters," Ava replied as the friends closed in on two classmates and a volatile witch moving towards an infamous building.

At the moment Tilly and Tom turned to face the cloaked figure, four of their classmates appeared from the bank of trees lining Horsel Hill, obviously locating their target via Follygrins, the circular notebook magically coming to life at the utterance of a name or place.

If anything, the sight of the others calmed Tilly and Tom's nerves, Ethan, Leah, Roan and Ava arriving to offer protection from the volatile witch. A bob of grey hair and high cheek bones were the two things Ava noticed, recognising the woman without being able to place her.

Olin and Katie appeared soon after, unnerved by the vision of their classmates in the company of a stranger. They'd heard the screams and general commotion outside Wimples, having no idea what had happened, although the sight of the sudden gathering on Horsel Hill suggested a possible explanation.

"Lovely afternoon, don't you think?" came the first words from the temperamental witch. "A perfect day for discovery."

None of group replied, focusing on preparing defensive spells just in case. Although only four of them had witnessed the strangulation spell outside Wimples, *all* of them sensed the air of menace surrounding the woman.

"Sofina Blin," the woman offered, inhaling deeply as she did.

Ethan and Leah exchanged a glance, wondering when the sudden attack was going to happen, but nothing more than friendly smiles followed, the large veins on her hands catching Ava's eye.

Ethan knew this was probably linked to a remedy, maybe one taken to heal battle scars — the thought of battle making him more interested by the minute. Successful graduation meant a life as a Society soldier to Ethan, already deciding faculty life wasn't for him.

He wanted to *use* charms not create them, send artefacts

flying towards the enemy rather than studying them. School was never his thing — action was — and he got the feeling Sofina Blin was of the same mind: a witch who whispered secret spells above ground was the sort of magician Ethan wanted to know. Subtle sorcery was the principle of all things S.P.M.A. after all.

"The *event* some of you witnessed earlier is an example of what happens to magicians with loose tongues," Sofina Blin explained, clicking her fingers to release sparks of light. "It had to be dealt with discreetly, of course, but dealt with nonetheless."

"That was a *student* you choked?" Roan asked, realising how far the Society would go to protect their secret world.

"An *ex* student who has thrown away the chance of a lifetime. You must remember that you are being watched at *every* turn. *Every* street corner and *every* Society space you enter. This will remain the case until you fall or fly. Ultimately, magical living will get the better of some of you, tempting you to share what you've learnt. A choking spell was the best she could hope for."

"The best?" Olin queried, wondering what he'd missed.

This caused the smile to fade from Sofina Blin's face, the green eyes sparkling with intensity. "Yes, the best Olin Zucklewick, and we all know what the worst outcome will be."

"A trip across Quibbs Causeway where the Mantzils wait," Olin added, more attuned to the risks of their trial.

"Not quite but something of a similar ilk," their eccentric companion replied. "More fitting to your age and inexperience."

"So, not as bad as slow death," Ethan added with a touch of sarcasm.

"No, a friendlier form of torture," Sofina replied with a

strange smile, making the students uneasy for the first time. "But enough of choking fits and potential pain lying ahead of you. It's time to turn to the task at hand. Does anyone know what the building behind us is called?"

"The Sylent," Leah replied as her black hair lifted in the wind. "A place where dark magic was studied years ago."

"Leading to the hunt for The Terrecet," Tilly added, stepping back when Sofina spun on her heels suddenly, pointing towards the brooding building dominating Horsel Hill.

"And now you have a hunt of your own, but like all trials certain obstacles have been put in place."

"What are we hunting?" Tom asked, feeling uneasy at the mention of The Terrecet: the lethal artefact his infamous uncle became obsessed with.

"A prize that will come in handy later on."

"One prize?"

"A prize for each of you, stored in separate locations in Society Square."

"What's the obstacle?" Katie asked, already thinking of the fastest way to get back to Society Square without being seen.

"Each prize needs to be found at night, and you can't be seen entering or leaving the building."

"So, we have to be invisible at all times?" Ava posed, her tall frame tensing at the thought of failing again.

"Only when above ground. Once inside your establishment, you are free to move as you wish. There will be other obstacles once inside. You have one hour to locate your prize: 9-10 p.m. If you fail in either returning or locating your prize, your days of magical living are numbered.

Oh, one other thing. You are well aware that captors

roam Society Square at night: a criminal group living off petty crime. If you happen to fall into their hands, your bags will be packed when you return to The Cendryll. One child has already failed and The Orium Circle want to accelerate things now.

The question of how young is too young is the point of this trial. Are you old enough to navigate above-ground streets at night? Can you operate alone when expectation rests on your shoulders. Most importantly, do you have the intuition required to solve problems when necessary? After all, if you can't maintain peace in plain sight, what good are you to us?"

"So, don't get seen or captured?" Ethan stated for purposes of clarification.

"And bring back what is waiting to be discovered," Sofina replied with a strange smile, clicking her fingers again to release more sparks of light. "I would enjoy the afternoon above ground, because it might be your last."

With that, the woman who'd choked a witch-in-training into submission moved towards a brooding building, uttering a spell to vanish within its layers of protection, leaving eight students to puzzle over the mission at hand.

"So, we've got to find something in God knows where before God knows who grabs us," Roan stated, sitting on the grass as he did. "Not much to go on, is it?"

"It's nothing to go on," Ava replied, studying the bustling streets of Society Square from their high vantage point.

"Which is the point," Olin added — the astute boy with gifts the others craved. "We have to use what we know to solve the mystery."

"Like what?" Tilly queried, pushing her red hair behind her ears.

"Like a Follygrin?"

"How's that going to help? We could spend hours saying the names of random buildings, and we've only got an hour to find these things."

"So, we say two things," Olin explained, drawing the attention of the others. "The word 'prize' and 'location'."

"That's not how Follygrins work," Ethan countered, kicking at the grass with his feet. "You have to say a *specific* place or person."

"Do you?" Olin challenged. "That's what we've been taught, but the whole point of these trials is being able to think for ourselves. What other way is there of locating the prizes?"

"By waiting somewhere above-ground," Leah suggested, her gentle nature intensifying as a solution occurred to her. "On the church roof, for example. Somewhere that gives us a panoramic view of Society Square."

"Waiting for a sign," Katie added, her competitive spirit kicking in as she tied her blonde hair back. "Like a light going on in a building."

"Eight buildings," Roan added, feeling himself drawn to this idea. "Each light acting as a starting gun, firing us into action."

"And then we head for the building in question," Katie added before stumbling across a problem, "except we won't know which building is linked to us."

"Unless the lights glow in the colour of our penchant stones," Olin added, realising his idea of using a Follygrin was less sophisticated than Leah's.

"So, we've got a plan to start on the church roof?" Ethan checked, enjoying how his classmates worked as a team: unity a principle that had been drilled into them.

"Yep," came the collective nod from the others.

"Then one hour to prove ourselves," Ethan added, sensing that a whole world was waiting for them in the above-ground establishments full of excited shoppers ... a world which would come to a standstill as the business stopped trading for the day ... until the time came to hunt for prizes that would determine their future.

7
MERCURIAL LEARNING

The evening light fell over Society Square as the allotted time arrived, the buildings resting in darkness. The church roof looked as it always did, empty of visitors who sometimes climbed to the top for some peace and quiet.

Perception wasn't always reality though, the current reality being eight students waiting behind invisibility charms, hoping their theory of a signal appearing within the buildings being right.

Katie posed the theory of coloured lights turning inside certain buildings, lights reflecting the colours of their penchant stones. If this didn't happen, they would have already lost time, but there was no other way of knowing where to search, or at least not one they could think of.

The dreaded captors were also roaming the streets, doing their best to stay in the shadows as the evening black-market trading began. Artefacts and remedies would change hands in secret spaces, coming to life when the above-ground world retired ... places like The Blind Horsemen, The Weary Winzer and others.

The places the students *really* wanted to go to were off limits, like The Shallows and The Royisin Heights, but they were located beyond The Society Sphere and anyone found transgressing this boundary faced automatic expulsion.

For now, trials to test their skill and wit continued, the first taste of danger being the questionable characters peering up at the church roof ... as if the captors knew all about the evening competition.

"What if we get kidnapped?" Roan asked, looking a little uneasy within their protective blanket.

"I doubt anyone's going to kidnap us," Ava replied. "The captors are part of the Society after all."

"Hanging on to Society living, you mean," Olin countered, his diminutive frame standing between Tilly and Tom. "They haven't done enough to get kicked out, but it's a fine line my dad always says."

"So, what threat do they pose if they're not going to kidnap us?" Tilly asked.

"To force us off track," Ethan suggested, "doing whatever they can to keep us away from the prizes we need to gather."

"Why?"

"Because that's the name of the game, isn't it? Proving we can handle a bit of danger on the way."

"Well, I'm up for a bit of danger," Katie added, rubbing her hands as the first light came on inside a shop opposite — Follygrin's — the shop that hid Society artefacts within less impressive objects.

To make sure Katie's theory was right, the others waited for more lights to appear, smiling when they did ... red, blue, orange, pink and purple lights glowing in the windows of familiar establishments ... Tallis & Crake, Wimples, Merrymopes, Cribbe & Corrow, Helping Hand, Pat's Cafe and The Spinning Shoe.

"Good luck," Ethan said as he uttered 'Bildin', generating a rope of light he grabbed onto.

Still protected within a glimmering curtain of light, the others did the same, preparing to swing into action. They knew the importance of not being seen going in or out of the buildings, so the Verum Veras charm remained intact, shimmering dust surrounding them as they glided through the air on glimmering ropes, swinging in various directions until they landed on the roof of their chosen building.

The sense of risk was obvious to them all, including the level of trust given to them. One mistake could lead to exposure and although there were ways of dealing with such errors, it would lead to unwanted rumour and speculation. They couldn't fail, Ava knew as she landed on top of The Spinning Shoe. It was time to prove their magical worth or return to mundane living.

With the utterance of 'Entrinius', Ava vanished through the roof, using a flight charm to ease her towards the main part of the shop — a building crammed with colourful shoes that acted as weapons to the uninvited. Thankfully, Ava was invited so didn't have to worry about heels turning into daggers.

The real problem was how to locate the prize determining her future in the S.P.M.A. *It could be anywhere,* Ava knew as she tip-toed through the shop, careful not to brush against any of the heels sticking out. The Spinning Shoe was where above-ground women came to get a 'lift', something unexplainable about the footwear immediately improving the person's mood.

Magic was the source of the mood enhancement, of course, another touch of wonder to add a little colour in an otherwise grey existence. It was exactly this existence the students feared returning to, each of them vanishing through the roof of a Society building.

The first stage of the trial had gone to plan, working out how to identify the buildings before activating magical travel without being seen. In some ways, that was the easy part, Roan knew, as he landed in the trading lane within Tallis & Crake ... the four pathways leading to the central trading space laying in darkness.

Usually buzzing with witches and wizards eager to trade artefacts, the wooden stools lining the trading lane sat empty, the drawers facing the stools making no offerings at such a late hour. The bartering box situated at the end of the trading lane provided no clues either, leaving Roan to conclude one thing: the need to sit at each stool, hoping one of the drawers presented him with the prize he was seeking.

Ethan found himself sitting in a booth in Merrymopes, smiling when the brass bell rang, signalling a descent to The Revolving Room below. He'd have to dial in once he reached the centre of the spinning structure, having no idea *where* to dial. The S.P.M.A. was made up of *hundreds* of realms and the prize could be anywhere, but the rules were simple: success or a sudden exit.

While Ethan made his way to The Revolving Room, the remaining classmates navigated their way through familiar buildings, Katie helping herself to a handful of sweets in Wimples, wondering if the prize was hidden in one of the jars lining the shelves.

It was their first real test with no adults present, a sense of freedom tinged with a touch of unease. After all, they were still young and unaccustomed to evening travel, but that was the least of their worries as movements formed around them ... in each of the buildings where a prize was hidden ... movements suggesting they had company.

Ava jumped as the heels shot out into spikes, stopping inches away from her tall figure. Her reaction was speedy, activating the Velinis charm just in time, the bubble of protection saving her from a catalogue of wounds. Olin was battling with a rising tide of water in Follygrin's, while Tom found himself staring into a mirror in Helping Hand.

Each had a journey ahead of them and a team of Society adults willing them on, Jacob studying a floating piece of parchment in his fifth-floor quarters, whispering instructions at the moving illustrations decorating the surveillance device, known as a Panorilum.

"Use your penchants," Jacob whispered as Olin finally worked this out, using his penchant ring to generate enough light to locate an exit, the small circles dotted on the walls expanding into tunnels, draining the space of water and allowing Olin to continue on.

Sipping a mug of hot Liqin — the remedy to clear his senses — Jacob looked up as Casper and Philomeena Renn walked into his study, coming along to offer company to a young man conditioned for isolation.

"Looks like I'll have a small class tomorrow," Jacob said as Ava jumped at the shuddering sound of more heels snapping into spikes.

"Have faith, Jacob," Casper replied, clicking his fingers to release a shower of light above the floating parchment. "They still have fifty minutes to go and company to help them, if necessary."

"It's too soon."

"It's always too soon," Philomeena replied, sitting on the leather chair opposite Jacob, ever resplendent in all black, "but it's necessary. With one student almost exposing our world earlier, The Orium Circle is losing patience. No more simple lessons on charms and remedies; it's time to assess capabilities and move on."

"It feels like we're setting them up to fail," Jacob added, his tall frame gaining a degree of elegance as he got older. "They've got nothing to go on."

"You had nothing to go on, but still solved the puzzle to save our world."

"With a little help."

"And your students will have help where necessary, but help isn't always going to be on hand, something they have to learn. We maintain peace by managing malice, something your sister knows only too well."

"Probably out saving the world again," Jacob replied with a smile, the thought of his sister flying through the skies bringing a smile to his face. A legendary Fire Witch, Guppy had promised to visit him soon, taking a break from protective duties.

"You miss it," Philomeena added, studying the moving illustrations of Jacob's class as the quest continued, "venturing through The Society Sphere with Guppy."

"Yes and no," Jacob replied, leaning closer to the floating parchment when Tom stepped through the cubicle door in Helping Hand, entering a grey land known as Sad Souls where giants waited to lead him on. "I miss being with Guppy but not the battle scars."

"Peaceful living gets tiresome after a while," Casper added, crossing his legs on the leather chair opposite his sister. "You'll get the bug again soon, probably when one of your students makes their first mistake."

"Which is right about now," Jacob added, standing at the sight of Roan falling off a stool in the trading lane as drawers flew out of their compartments ... drawers typically offering simple trades but now releasing the obstacles

Sofina Blin warned the students of ... obstacles in the form of white insects that whipped into the air.

"A return to action," Casper commented with a smile, remaining calm at the sight of Roan lifted into the air by the insects, wrapping strings of white around his neck as he struggled to free himself.

"As one of my students gets *strangled*."

"*Transported*, Jacob ... to where they need to be."

"Well, I don't want a dead student on my watch so if you don't mind," Jacob added, taking off his Society tie as he hurried towards the door near the window: a Perium taking him to the trading lane of Tallis & Crake and a student on the verge of a strange crucifixion.

"Some are more impressive than others," Philomeena stated as the door closed in the room, "and some leave questions to be answered."

"They're going to keep us busy over the next few months," Casper commented, "pushing the boundaries of accepted wizardry."

"The nature of childhood."

"Returning us to the question of limits," Casper added. "What do we limit underage magicians to without returning to the secrecy of the past?"

"A question they're likely to answer themselves," Philomeena replied, enjoying a quiet moment with her brother. "Has Kaira been in touch?"

"Not recently, which means she's close to home."

"Assuming she views the S.P.M.A. as home."

"She always will," Casper added, uttering 'Flori' as a daisy appeared in the palm of his hand. "It's where her life truly began, and where it will end."

"Well, she has plenty of living to do and we have students to rescue," Philomeena added, touching the floating parchment to magnify two images: Olin taking cover from a collapsing upper floor in Follygrins, while Tilly fought off an attack of flying penchants bursting from the shelves of Cribbe & Corrow.

"Time to lend a helping hand," Casper stated, spinning the image of Olin into a ball, blowing on it until it formed into stairs. "Shall we?" he added with wry humour, stepping onto the stairs with his sister before disappearing from view.

WITH THE EVENING TRIAL IN FULL SWING, VARYING VISIONS OF mercurial learning were offering entertainment in Society establishments. Some questioned the wisdom of introducing magic to children so young, while the majority recognised the essence of childhood had served them so well recently.

Ultimately, The Orium Circle had made a decision, the faculty of lawmakers having the final say as always. Although little had changed within the S.P.M.A. much had been lost in recent years, including the lives of Society soldiers who'd sacrificed themselves to maintain peace.

The better prepared future generations were, the less likely battle would break out again within and beyond the Society, meaning a life of peaceful wonder could be maintained for many years to come. First, hard lessons had to be learnt in the safe confines of Society buildings, including how to navigate sudden swarms of sorcery.

Touch and timing were at the heart of the evening's lesson, a skill coming naturally to some more than others. It was something no magic spell could provide, the critical intuition needed to navigate a world of wonder.

With Society Square maintaining a facade of normality, the drama intensified in eight of its buildings, collapsing rooms, flying penchants and white insects acting as hangmen pushing The Fateful Eight to the limit. Wherever the prizes were, there was going to be a lot of carnage before they were found, although this wasn't a concern to Society onlookers.

The Repellia charm returned all things to their natural state, allowing for the buildings to collapse in on themselves whilst the external facade was unchanged. Olin was the student faced with a collapsing upper floor, having survived a rising tide of water in a secret chamber hidden within Follygrin's.

Had he known the history of the Society shop, he would have been better prepared, but anticipation was central to this wizarding trial. With Casper Renn appearing behind him, Olin spun within a Velinis charm, the green bubble of protection shielding him from the collapsing debris.

How the building remained upright was obvious, a Disineris charm used to disintegrate a specific part ... the part holding the prize Olin had to find as the clock ticked down on Society survival.

"The Fora charm!" Casper called out, flicking his Vaspyl into an umbrella as he walked through the collapsing room, like a man on an evening stroll with nothing on his mind. "Quickly, before the floor evaporates from view."

Olin did as instructed, shouting 'FORA' to create a wider force field of protection ... an expanding curtain of light that halted the shower of debris ... just as the floor *did* evaporate under his feet, leaving Casper to look on as Olin fell into the main shop floor, the glass towers lining the rooms crammed with strange objects.

Within one of them was the prize he sought, but *which one*? Olin thought, watching as Casper floated down, using the umbrella to guide his flight.

It was obvious why Casper had appeared, Olin thought, recognising he needed a helping hand. Whether this would go against him was uncertain, but there was no time to dwell on ifs or maybes — the clock was ticking and he had less than forty minutes to find a prize in a maze of artefacts.

Added to this, he was standing in a shop facing onto Founders' Quad, meaning he couldn't just become invisible during the search. That would *definitely* get him expelled, so he turned to Casper for guidance.

"Mirriul," Casper uttered, raising his arms towards the shop windows.

As he did, a strange film rested over the glass, presenting an image of a silent shop resting in darkness. There was no sign of the two of them in the reflection, meaning another protective layer had been provided.

"Now, it's time for the test to begin," Casper stated, brushing dust off his silver suit as he stood by the shop counter. "There are hundreds of artefacts in each cabinet. The question is which one will be your salvation?"

"My what?"

"Your salvation. Your lucky charm and guiding light. The prize you seek encompasses all these things and more, and you only have thirty-eight minutes to locate it."

"And you're not going to help me?"

"My job is to guide you."

"Well, can I have some guidance?"

"Of course ... start looking."

With Casper overseeing Olin's hunt, Jacob had his work cut out with Roan who had descended into panic, striking out at the white insects lifting him up by his throat.

"Relax!" Jacob instructed as he stepped onto the trading lane, looking up at Roan who was doing the opposite.

Kicking his legs out as he struggled for breath, Roan gestured for help with his hands, trying to fire out at the storm of white insects enacting the second strangulation of the day.

"Stop fighting back!" Jacob called again, knowing he could only guide. "The white insects are putting you in position."

With that, Roan stopped his struggle, partly out of desperation. He felt himself losing consciousness, realising he'd fallen into the trap that had been set for him, assuming anything engaging him was a threat. This was a trial, after all, and death wasn't part of failure — or at least that's what he assumed — so he let his body go limp as the pressure around his throat eased.

"Place your arms through the strings of white around your neck," Jacob called up to Roan, uttering 'Spintz' to illuminate his stricken student with a shower of light.

Now calmer and following his teacher's lead, Roan inhaled before focusing on Jacob.

"Now, point your arms towards the ceiling and wait for the strings of light to converge. When they do, you'll have the location of your prize."

Roan nodded his understanding, still struggling to speak after over reacting to an unfamiliar creature. He was still too slow when it mattered most, failing in Heaven's Chamber and struggling without Jacob's guidance. Maybe he wasn't cut out for Society living after all, the curse of his infamous uncle coming back to haunt him.

"*There*," Jacob stated, pointing to the spot on the ceiling marked by the white strings, courtesy of the creatures known as doveflies. "Now, obliterate the ceiling and catch what falls."

With that, Roan gathered his strength, closing his eyes before shouting 'DISINERIS', shattering the high-beamed ceiling in search of his own salvation.

8
SOCIETY TRIALS

With Roan and Olin beginning their search for a personal prize, Ava continued to manoeuvre her way through dagger-like shoes closing in on her. Invited or not, the interior of The Spinning Shoe was reacting as if she was an unwelcome visitor, obviously part of the plan to test her mercurial movements.

As shadows passed the windows on the street outside, Ava sensed the need to accelerate the search. A Mirriul charm protected her from view, the spell providing a vision of calm to onlookers, but that didn't mean captors roaming the evening streets weren't aware of her presence inside. After all, they were aware of a presence on the church roof at the start of the trial, meaning they were obviously part of this strange game.

It wasn't a game Ava could afford to come last in, realising she'd had too many false starts on being selected as one of The Fateful Eight. She often wondered how the other classes were doing, trained in the faculties spread across the S.P.M.A. One thing was for certain, they had phenomenal teachers in Jacob, Casper and Philomeena Renn, so if she didn't make it she'd only have herself to blame.

"Thirty minutes," Ava whispered, secretly hoping someone would appear to help her.

When someone *did* appear, she smiled a sigh of relief at the familiar face, resplendent in black.

"You've managed without a scratch so far," Philomeena Renn stated as the dagger-like shoes retracted into more welcoming forms. "Now, you've got to sense the environment you're in."

"How do you mean?" Ava asked, her ruby-red bubble of protection glowing in the dark space.

"There are some things magic can't teach you, Ava, and one of them is sensibility. In essence, it's picking up on the *tone* of things — be that emotional, physical or psychological."

"Like reading energy, you mean?"

"Yes, precisely that."

"And that's what I need to do to find the prize?" Ava asked, happy to see the killer heels retract into the wooden shelves

"Yes, meaning you need to deactivate the Velinis charm."

Ava hesitated at this thought, standing as tall as her legendary teacher on the shop floor, resting in darkness. The top of the building was decorated with an enormous spinning shoe, making Ava wonder if the prize was hidden in there. It was too obvious but not something she could rule out — a thought that drove her on as she studied the staircase resting in darkness.

"What if I get stabbed by more jutting heels?"

"We have remedies for such things," Philomeena replied, her flawless, caramel skin and striking features giving her a regal look. "Injuries are par for the course, Ava, and certainly something to get used to if you want a life in our world. *Sensibility* is what we're truly testing tonight, so trust me when I say rely on *pure instinct not* the magic you've been taught.

Magical learning can lead to reliance — the assumption that it's a solution to all things. Of course, it isn't. Bravery, intelligence and *intuition* are the centrepieces of sorcery, so be brave."

With that, Ava glanced at the ring on the middle finger of her left hand … the penchant that infused her veins with a superpower … magic in many forms that would only take her so far. What she needed now was a spark of an idea … a *sense* of the energy of things … particularly the force field emanating from a prize she was desperate to claim.

She couldn't go back to above-ground living, she just *couldn't,* so that meant following her teacher's advice, focusing on gifts she was yet to realise … gifts that led her on to a discovery keeping her dreams alive. As she stepped onto the stairs, another shadow passed by the window, but this time it didn't distract her from the job at hand.

The Society stragglers moving through Founders' Quad were the captors she'd seen earlier, roaming between black market establishments under the cover of darkness. She couldn't be seen or caught on this mission, turning her mind away from the consequences of either.

Fear served no purpose now, she knew, creeping up the stairs with her eyes on the shoes resting in the wooden shelves … shoes of various colours and designs, shifting with each step she took … remaining true to the principle of bravery Philomeena had pointed out. She didn't care about being injured if it meant finding the prize, hiding somewhere in a silent space housing a portal of a different kind.

With Philomeena nowhere to be seen now, Ava breathed a sigh of relief as she reached the top of the staircase, free of injury. Now she was looking at a brass pole in the room to her left — a glimmering pole that she assumed led to the enormous, red shoe decorating the roof.

"Well, here goes nothing," she whispered as she stepped towards the pole, expecting it to lift her upwards as she made contact with it.

Grabbing on had no effect, though, until a hand appeared out of nowhere, causing Ava to scream. The figure of the young girl appearing in the darkness was almost ghostlike, until she smiled at Ava: a smile of welcome to a realm described in various Society books.

"We haven't got long," the girl stated, holding out her right hand.

Ava took it without hesitation, aware she needed all the help she could get.

SENREIYA WAS A WONDER OF LIGHT — A REALM OF SUCH natural beauty it was hard to process all at once. A field of blue birds and a rainbow sky were the first things Ava captured, before the volcanic structures towering towards the sky dominated her vision. The swinging bridges connected to the towers were decorated with birds known as Jacqus.

Ava knew little about Senreiya other than the fact Jacob had been here before. It was a realm under siege in a previous war, the carpet of colour decorating the sky linked to the magical axis of an entire universe. There was little time to process it all let alone venture through it, Ava shocked to hear she only had fifteen minutes to find the object marking her success in the trial.

"Time moves differently here," the girl explained, walking alongside her in a white dress.

Other children played in the field, appearing then disappearing as they practised vanishing charms. It was a training ground of sorts, although more natural in feel and principle — childhood of a different kind.

"Can you help me?" Ava asked as the sun shimmered down on them.

"In a way. Watch the rhythm of the swinging bridges; the clue is there."

With that, the girl stepped away with a smile, joining her friends in their own pursuit of perfecting spells, leaving Ava to wonder if sensibility wasn't something carved into her DNA. As far as she could tell, each bridge swung in unison … a synchronised touch to a stunning landscape … until one bridge slowed … the only sign she had with less than fifteen minutes to go.

As Ava found the clue she needed and Roan obliterated the roof of the trading lane, Olin continued his search within the glass cabinets in Follygrin's — the unremarkable shop hiding spectacular artefacts amongst everyday objects. *How* he was supposed to find a particular gift still puzzled him, the realisation that Casper Renn was only a guide, standing by the shop counter as Olin's panic got the better of him.

"I'm not going to find it!" Olin said as the ring on his left hand vibrated.

"You just need to make the connection," Casper advised,

confident the Mirriul charm continued to protect them from prying eyes.

Captors and above-ground stragglers were no concern for a man skilled in sorcery, but they were distracting Olin from the task at hand.

"What connection?" Olin asked, catching a glimpse of the church tower and the faint sign of activity on top.

Someone had already been successful in their attempt, he thought, probably Katie who *loved* winning. He was usually the one to find a way out of tricky situations, but not tonight it seemed.

"The connection between your penchant and the object you seek," Casper explained, moving away from the shop counter. "The vibration will get stronger the closer you get so shut out everything else, including what's happening outside, and sense the target. You've got less than ten minutes."

As Olin closed his eyes, hoping this would help him detect the object, Casper took a small book from his jacket pocket. Throwing it into the air, he watched as the book unfolded into a large piece of parchment, the moving illustrations forming on it providing an overview of the students' progress.

Like Follygrins, Panorilums offered insight into Society movements, the movements of The Fateful Eight being the current concern. With less than ten minutes to go, only one person had found the prize awaiting them — Tilly Flint — who was watching from the church roof.

Hidden in a Verum Veras charm, Tilly searched the seven buildings decorated in soft light, urging her classmates on.

"*Come on,*" she whispered as she studied the glass object in her hand.

It was a baton-shaped object with flecks of gold swimming in its centre. What it did was uncertain although Tilly was sure it was the prize she had to gather, mainly because she'd come across it by accident, using the 'Exhibius' charm to activate the illustrated window in Cribbe & Corrow: the place where penchants were acquired.

The charm had revealed an endless corridor in the illustrated window, Tilly realising she needed to step through the window to continue the search. Logic dictated that this would lead to a fatal fall to her death, but logic had little place in the S.P.M.A.

The decision had proven to be a sound one, Tilly pushing her hand through the liquid glass to test she was stepping onto solid ground ... the endless hallway she eventually stepped into leading her past numerous doors until her penchant bracelet vibrated ... suggesting she was closing in on her target.

Instinct did the rest as Tilly stood in front of a closed door, feeling her penchant bracelet heat up as she placed her hand on the brass handle. Something told her not to open the door though ... the memory of the single shaft of light she first saw in the illustrated window causing her to pause and look up ... at the lamp blinking above the door.

The lamp emanated a ringing sound as she reached up to touch it, shocked by the surge of power flooding through her body as she did ... a surge so powerful it sent her crashing to the floor ... the baton-shaped object clasped in her right hand. She knew it was a weapon of some sort, sensing it would be needed at some point in the future.

As the lights went out in the seven buildings, Tilly stood alone on the church roof, turning the glass artefact in her right hand as the clock struck ten: the signal to return to The Cendryll.

She found the others at The Seating Station, buzzing with excitement as they discussed their adventures with each other. Jacob was standing on the periphery, talking to Sofina Blin who turned at the sight of Tilly returning. The grey-haired witch had introduced herself on Horsel Hill earlier, friendly in manner and blunt in tone.

Whoever got seen or caught would be a goner, Sofina had explained, turning towards The Sylent once the rules of the trial had been clarified. Now, she was in The Cendryll to judge the outcome of the task ... more senior than Jacob and less fun ... making Tilly wonder if she *had* acquired that right thing after all.

None of her classmates seemed overly concerned, though, Leah offering a smile as Tilly sat alongside her — the red-headed girl who still hadn't made up her mind about her future. Unlike the others, she missed the above-ground world to some degree, particularly her friends who ignored her when she appeared on Founders' Quad.

They had been angry at the way she'd just *vanished* from their lives, unhappy with the explanation they received, finally deciding some friends just moved on. Tilly *had* moved on, of course, but not in the way of abandonment or betrayal.

She'd felt pressure from her parents once she'd processed the incredible news, that they worked in a 'special place where special things happened'. They introduced the proposal in stages, saying very little about magic until it became obvious they were hiding something.

"It has to be seen to be understood," her dad had said, offering the nervous smile he always did when her mum was pushing for something. "It's a chance of a lifetime, love."

Well, he'd been right about that, events accelerating until the day of induction three months ago, Tilly entering Cribbe & Corrow with her parents and taking a step behind the baize curtain, watching as Morlan Corrow placed a wooden case on the table in the centre of the room.

"Your penchant, Miss Flint," the odd man had explained, bowing as he did so. "What you will need to *go on*."

And on she went, leading her to this very point, sitting in The Seating Station with a group of new friends, wondering what meaning lay behind the evening events. It was more than finding a prize, she felt, judging from the look on Jacob's face. It was about what had been *offered* as if the objects had found the students, not the other way around.

It had been a test of alignment, Tilly decided, making her wonder why the glass baton had *found her*, and what it would eventually lead to.

"What did you find?" Leah asked with a smile, studying the object in Tilly's hand.

"This," she replied, feigning a lack of interest.

"Mine sort of *attached itself* to me," Leah explained, lifting her right arm to display the weave of silver running along it. "I don't know how you get it off."

"You don't," Sofina Blin replied, getting the attention of the class. "The weave will fade into your skin in a few hours, returning when you need it most."

"Okay," Leah uttered with a look of puzzlement.

"You were all successful in your mission, claiming the prize set out for you," Sofina added. "Now, you have to understand the power bestowed upon you. How to harness it and contain it."

"So, what are they?" Roan asked, studying the gold pin that pierced his hand.

"Weapons," Jacob replied with an uneasy look.

"So, we *are* going to fight in battle," Ethan stated, smiling at the thought of this.

"Only a battle with yourself," Sofina Blin replied as the moon appeared in the skylight.

"So, we're *not* using the weapons?" Ava asked, still reeling from a dramatic visit to Senreiya where a swing bridge had catapulted her towards a multi-coloured sky.

"You'll be guided by them," Jacob explained, looking like he needed his sleep. Moving towards the lift, their young teacher added, "Well done on acquiring what you needed to; the rest will become clear in time. Now, off to bed."

"So, we've got weapons that aren't weapons, and we're *not* fighting any battles except the one with ourselves," Katie stated as Jacob and Sofina Blin made their way towards the lift behind The Seating Station.

"Why not just give us the objects?" Tom asked, feeling uneasy with the idea of an artefact holding powers he didn't understand.

"Because we needed to be drawn to them," Tilly stated, remembering how the lamp buzzed in Cribbe & Corrow, before she found herself on the ground with a glass baton in her hand. "They needed to discover something in us, something we don't understand yet."

"Spoken like a true philosopher," Katie commented with a degree of bitterness, wondering why she only had a golden lace as a prize.

"Tilly's right," Ethan added, tapping his foot at the thought of finding out things about himself he didn't know. Was he good enough? Brave enough? Skilled enough to survive? Would he even know how to activate the power within the smoking pendant in his left hand, reflecting the orange hue of his penchant stone.

"Well, what did everyone else find?" Ava asked, keen to know more about her classmates' evening quests, mainly because she was worried her discovery was more a warning than a weapon.

9
QUIET TIME

As The Fateful Eight poured over the prizes gathered, Jacob stood by the window of his fifth-floor quarters, listening to Sofina Blin's reminder of what to expect next. Studying his reflection as the talkative witch droned on, Jacob wondered if a life of teaching was ageing him prematurely. He looked drawn in the face and paler than usual, his dark hair in need of attention.

What he thought would be peaceful Society living was turning into anything but, the students' hyperactivity far more draining than he could have imagined. Then there'd been the girl who'd received the choking spell this morning — Ellie Zucklewick — a bright spark with a big talent and even bigger mouth.

The mother played along with the enactment, a Society elder who knew punishment was forthcoming. She could do little more than panic as Sofina whispered the choking spell: the consequence of a loose tongue. The Removilis charm would take care of the rest, sending the girl back to above-ground living none the wiser, leaving a mother to mourn an opportunity lost.

The mistake had changed the tone within Society faculties up and down the land, Scribberals rattling with concern as discussions on how to proceed began. Abandoning the experiment was one of the proposals, although The Orium Circle dismissed this straight away.

The faculty responsible for law making made their position clear: all students would have the same chance afforded to them as the adults; however, extra precautions would be put in place to avoid fatal injury. It was a simple way of sorting the destined from the deadwood, The Orium Circle argued, leading to the evening trial that had just been completed.

The key aspect of the trial was the principle of pursuit and uniqueness, making the students believe they were aligned to their prizes, chosen and therefore special. Those with fragile egos would begin to obsess over the power hidden within their object, keen to unravel the source of magic bestowed upon them.

Others would dwell on mastering the art of sorcery, leaving a fateful few who would reach the heights necessary for permanent residency in the S.P.M.A.

Sofina had arrived to put across her views on the ones already failing, in her eyes, annoying Jacob with her judgements and incessant talking as she clattered cups in the small kitchen, looking for something more interesting than tea.

"Half of them didn't really find the prize; it ended up being given to them."

"I know," Jacob replied, looking out of the window onto Founders' Quad.

"Meaning we already know who's likely to fail."

"Meaning you've already decided who you *think* will fail."

"Same thing."

"Not really."

"So sensitive these days, Jacob," Sofina added, shrugging off her grey cloak as she rested on the leather sofa adjacent to the window. "You need to spend a little more time in Rebel's Rest; I know Ilina would like to see you."

Mention of the elegant girl who Jacob secretly admired brought a lighter tone to proceedings.

"I've barely got any energy when the day's over."

"Love has a way of lifting the spirits," Sofina replied, handing Jacob a vial of red liquid.

"Have some of this."

Deciding not to question what it was, Jacob gulped the remedy down, thankful for anything to take the edge off the day. Teaching was a *lot* harder than he'd imagined, especially judging when the students were ready to progress. Simple errors could be costly, leading to permanent injuries and shattered dreams.

"It's time for extensive tests."

"I know. I just hope I've prepared them well enough."

"Of course you have," Sofina replied, studying the glowing gem in the brooch decorating her grey cloak."

"Let's hope no one gets killed this time."

"Have some faith, Jacob. Every activity is meticulously planned, ensuring danger is present but *managed*. It's important that the students feel a mixture of fear and wonder, helping them understand the fine balance of magical living. Those who make it will experience beauty and burden, so they need to have adequate experience of both."

"You mentioned some teaching in The Ghost Quarter," Jacob prompted, thinking of a part of The Society Sphere he rarely ventured to. It had a strange energy and even stranger architecture ... buildings in perpetual motion ... changing their shape and structure as if restless spirits controlled them.

"Yes, the section of The Society Sphere most fitting to our aims. The buildings will provide the traps we need — harmless, of course."

"They'll also take the students into unknown territory," Jacob added, looking out over Founders' Quad as a headache grew.

"Par for the course," Sofina replied, sitting on a kitchen stool. "The necessary boundaries are in place, ensuring no student is able to go beyond The Society Sphere, but there are plenty of adventures to be had along the way. We want to maintain the fun of magical living, avoiding any sense that Society living is all about strife."

"Well, it has been recently."

"Only by choice, to a degree. Guppy and her Night Ranger crew accepted a mission in the sky realms, and you felt the need to join them."

"Brotherly duty," Jacob countered, turning to look at the grey-haired witch with a propensity for choking spells. "Let's make sure things don't get out of hand."

"It won't come to that."

"It usually does."

"Jacob, you need to trust the process. Everything has been planned. After all, if it was easy anyone could succeed in our world. The students were chosen because of certain traits: characteristics that run in each of the families."

"Special gifts that will help us in the future."

"Yes."

"So, it's really a case of separating the loyal from the questionable."

"Indeed it is," Sofina replied, blowing on her hand to release a wisp of light.

The light floated towards Jacob's stationary figure, preoccupied with something other than the progress of his class. He had another person on his mind, placing his hand on one of the window panes and uttering 'Exhibius'. As he did, an image of a familiar establishment came into view: Rebel's Rest.

Jacob smiled at the sight of Ilina enjoying the jovial atmosphere of a popular Society establishment. Situated in The Singing Quarter, Rebel's Rest drew the restless and raucous, the wood-panelled walls swinging open as more witches and wizards entered the crowded space.

As silver trays floated through the air, collecting and delivering drinks, a handful of regulars stood on the bar, belting out popular songs ... the manic energy of the place lifting the mood of whoever entered. It was the perfect place to forget Society business.

"There's more to life than Society duty," Sofina commented, moving over to the illustrated window. "It's not too late to join the party, Jacob."

As a dance broke out in Rebel's Rest, Jacob ran his hand across the window pane, deciding it was time for a little fun. The Fateful Eight were tucked away in their family quarters, discussing their discoveries excitedly. There would be much more to discover, including things about themselves.

In the end, mercurial living was a balance of magical training and acute intuition: a sixth sense which would be the distinguishing mark. For now, Jacob would make his own mark on the girl he'd been afraid to love, mainly due to his own insecurities. His mother had left a permanent mark: a scar of sorts that raised questions of intimacy.

He knew how to love gently but wasn't certain he could intensely, fully aware of the consequences of living with a distant mother. His mother was another story all together,

her isolated existence on the Society margins something he'd come to terms with. Loss had been the dominant emotion in recent years, Jacob knew, recognising the need to find balance within his life.

"You're right," Jacob replied, turning to give Sofina a smile as he stepped away from the illustrated window, moving towards the narrow door in the corner of the room.

Placing his hand on the brass door handle, he pulled it towards him and turned it. As gold letters appeared above the handle, he waited until *Rebel's Rest* appeared. When it did, he pushed the handle back in and pulled the door open, waving goodnight to Sofina as he closed the door behind him.

Standing in darkness for a moment, Jacob uttered 'Spintz' to release a shower of light — the very thing needed to locate the lamp above. He reached for the string to turn on the lamp, laughing as the floor rotated, sending him into a blizzard of noise and colour, creative charms fizzing around him as a familiar face appeared.

"Thank God," Ilina said as she reached for Jacob's hand, leading him towards the merriment. "I thought I'd never get rid of him."

"Who?" Jacob asked as he was spun into a dance.

"Grenville Mirch."

"Who?"

"Never mind," Ilina said, pulling Jacob closer as a new song broke out. "He's creepy to say the least."

"Obviously fallen for your charm."

"Something like that. Anyway, why so absent lately?"

"Society trials."

"Which don't run day and night."

"Teaching's a lot harder than I thought it would be."

"Then give it up and have some fun."

"I'm having fun now."

"So, do it more," Ilina commented, lifting her mauve dress as she swirled to the music.

"You sound like you've missed me," Jacob added, feeling Ilina's waist press into his.

"We've all missed you!" came the voice of Harvey — a round, red-faced friend of Ilina's with frenetic energy. "So, who's going to make the cut?" Harvey asked as he broke into a very bad robot dance, sweat pouring down his face."

"Too early to say," Jacob replied, keeping in time with Ilina as she pulled him closer, resting her head on his shoulder: a sign to keep his focus on a prize of his own.

"I've said Olin from the start," Jalem commented, the other colleague that made up Ilina's trio of friends.

Tall and handsome in a way, Jalem showed little interest in anything beyond his work, determined to be the youngest wizard to create a defensive charm. Other charms were less complicated, but defensive charms required many hours of research, followed by even more hours of practice.

"Ethan!" Harvey shouted as his robot dance continued amongst the crowd of rabble rousers. "All the style and grace of his grandfather, the legendary Weyen Lyell."

"Tilly will be the first to make the grade," Ilina added, her black handbag resting on her left wrist as the clapping began, turning a slow waltz into a more boisterous burst of activity. "She's got the touch."

"What touch?" Harvey asked, intrigued by a notion of a gifted witch in the mix.

"A touch that can't be taught," Ilina replied, leading Jacob towards the exit.

"Is Jacob going to get the touch now?" Harvey teased, offering Jacob a smile.

"I'll leave that to your imagination," Ilina replied with

her usual elegance, stepping into the cold night air with her boy wizard.

Imagination was the name of the game, Ilina knew, uttering 'Cympgus' to create a circle of blue light on the evening streets. As other archways of light glimmered into existence, she took Jacob's hand and led him through their portable Perium. It was a romantic trip of a different kind, moving between wondrous spaces to capture the S.P.M.A. in all its glory.

It was a way of Ilina showing Jacob what life could be like, without the constant burden of Society duty. Stunning places like Velerin's — the snow-globe-shaped restaurant in The Winter Quarter — and The Cathedral of Stars in The Illustrated Quarter.

Jacob thought of family when he took these visits, laughing more easily as he travelled with the girl who'd captured his attention. What would magical living feel like without a purpose? Without the need to give constantly? Would it feel richer or more hollow? Exhilarating or an echo of what had been?

The Illustrated Quarter was the location of choice, the buildings decorated by enormous pictures acting as Periums. Each illustration offered a vision of the wonder on offer, The Cathedral of Stars one of Ilina's favourite places.

Formed on a crossroads, each section of The Illustrated Quarter offered various delights, the sign post at the centre of the crossroads changing every few seconds. The illustrations changed as well, flicking new visions into life to excite and entice Society members.

It was the place Ilina took Jacob to take his mind off The Cendryll, the place he now called home. She knew how much the magical faculty meant to him, but also understood the consequences of Society duty, the faint scars on his neck and hands a reminder of this.

She often wondered would it take for him to step back from Society duty, wondering if she could commit to him if he didn't? Would he have to sacrifice as much as Casper and Philomeena in the end, and did he even want to? Questions Ilina decided to park as they walked through the glimmering space.

The Cathedral of Stars was a map of sorts, each star symbolising a unique aspect of the infinite universe of the S.P.M.A. On touching a star, it expanded into a representation of the space, a compass symbol hovering above it to demarcate its location.

"A world of wonder at your fingertips," Ilina said as they studied an unfamiliar realm called Orilin. "A realm formed of water, and then there's Kymul: the exploding realm."

"We'll travel there one day," Jacob promised, accepting the offer of Ilina's hand, wondering when love would trump duty.

"Sometimes one day never comes."

"It will."

"When The Fateful Eight have made their way?"

"Probably."

"Until another group of bright young things need you."

"You sound resentful."

"Maybe a little, but I'm happy for the moments we get."

"I wish it could be more."

"Then wish it into existence, Jacob Grayling," Ilina replied with a smile before kissing Jacob on the forehead.

"I struggle to let go."

"We all hold on to something," Ilina added as they walked through the glittering space.

"The Society saved me, Ilina."

"I know, but it doesn't need you to save *it*. You've done that once already."

"Where do you think this is?" Jacob asked as he touched a spinning star with his finger.

"Right here," Ilina replied, squeezing his hand. "The Illustrated Quarter."

"You like it here."

"It's romantic. It helps me to remember the normal things: the things that matter most."

"Love," Jacob uttered, tapping another star that spun into a realm covered in snow … The Winter Quarter … his sister's favourite part of The Society Sphere.

Guppy had found love early in life, committing to the boy born to fly: Conrad Kusp. Now it was Jacob's turn to balance Society living with matters of the heart: a balance he would find hard to strike as events unfolded.

10

PRIZES & PREPARATIONS

As Jacob pondered his own future in the cathedral of stars, The Fateful Eight were busy discussing the prizes they'd uncovered in various parts of The Cendryll. Roan, Ava and Olin were debating the purpose of the evening's events, tucked away in the third-floor quarters Ava shared with her dad. Henry Blin had prepared a midnight feast, realising sleep wasn't on the children's agenda at present.

"See how the glass cabinet almost trapped me in Follygrin's," Olin stated, pointing to the moving illustration on the Panorilum, a floating piece of parchment hanging in the centre of the room. "When I reached in to the search for the prize, I was sort of *pulled* in and before I knew it, I was surrounded by a sea of silver."

"Which is when you started to fall," Ava commented, pointing at the moment Olin sank into the sea of steel.

They'd learnt the art of viewing past events with the help of a Now-Then: a brass, spinning top. A Now-Then was normally used in the space the past event had occurred in, but in situations where multiple events needed to be viewed, it was attached to the top of a Panorilum, allowing the floating parchment to reveal what had gone before.

The trio studied the intricate illustrations, each one replaying their evening adventure as they battled through various traps and obstacles to uncover the required prize. The obstacles Olin faced included water, a collapsing room and an expanding glass cabinet – a cabinet leading him into an expanding realm of steel.

It took him a while to take in the shifting structure he'd been sucked into, steel artefacts raining down on either side of him, changing shape as they did while the ones under his feet tilted him in various directions. The drop was as sudden as the entrance, normal rules of space and time having little meaning where everything could be manipulated.

"That's when I saw it," Olin said, standing from his kneeling position in the centre of the room. "The one artefact that changed colour but not shape, just as I was sucked in again. Only this time, I used a Magneia charm to pull me out which is when things got more interesting."

"The artefact turning into an orb of light," Roan commented, glancing at the object in Olin's hand.

"Firing towards me as I closed in on it," Olin added, "which is when I realised the point of being pulled into the glass cabinet. The waterfall of steel was my arsenal, used to shield and move me into position."

"What made you think it was dangerous?" Ava queried, happy to relive their adventures in the safe confines of her dad's quarters.

"The way it hissed," Olin replied. "That's the only way I can explain it. I felt I needed to capture it to claim it; until that point I was its enemy."

"And you just *sensed* that?"

Olin grabbed another handful of sweets from the mountain of confectionary. "I suppose. It's the one thing I've got going for me: a sense of my surroundings. Let's face it, I haven't got height, physique or charm on my side."

"I think you're pretty charming," Roan joked, giving his classmate a friendly nudge.

"Thanks," Olin replied with a smile, happy to belong in a faculty without a parent to guide him.

His inclusion in The Fateful Eight was more complicated than the others, his parents reluctantly accepting the offer after weeks of being badgered by their only son. Spending the majority of their time running a Society establishment above-ground, Arthur and Esther Zucklewick saw no reason to disrupt tradition.

Olin, however, had other thoughts, deciding Society living was for him. His parents had explained that danger came with the territory despite peace being the aim, their son nodding along earnestly whilst his mind raced with visions of raging battles. He wanted to experience every thrill and thread of the vast, expanding universe of the S.P.M.A., the Society trials offering the chance to do just that.

"Which is why Casper was there to guide you," Ava's dad interjected, studying the small boy with a gift for sorcery. "All Society members are given guidance when needed, Olin, and there's no better guide than Casper Renn."

"It's weird how he *didn't* help in a way," Olin added, stuffing the sweets in his mouth.

"What do you mean?" Roan asked, sitting cross-legged between his friends.

Wishing he had Olin's sixth sense in all things magical, Roan was happy Ava had invited their classmate to their midnight feast. Olin was like Ava and Roan in some ways: an outsider with a fierce determination to succeed.

Unlike some of the others – Ethan and Katie particularly – he wasn't obsessed with winning at any cost, often helping others out when they floundered. Roan liked this quality in Olin, sensing he'd found a friend.

"Casper's silence was a statement of faith," Ava's dad added, secretly wishing he was free of family responsibilities, able to travel far and wide to places only whispered about behind closed doors. "It wasn't until you succeeded that you realised this."

"Which makes you a favourite," Ava added, offering her diminutive classmate a smile. "With Casper Renn on your side, how can you fail?"

Ava certainly wasn't a front runner at the moment, failing to ascend Heaven's Chamber and almost running out of time in Senreiya, the beautiful realm with a rainbow-coloured sky. In the end, she had to rely on the mercy of the Jacqus to lift her higher — the shimmering, blue birds carrying her to the top of the volcanic structures where her prize awaited her: a silver star spinning in the air.

The star darted back and forth, evading Ava's grasp and the power of the Magneia charm. It was a moment of intuition that finally drew the spinning artefact towards her, the utterance of 'Exhibius' causing the edges of the star to separate until the vision of a past moment appeared ... of Ava taking the hand of a girl in The Spinning Shoe.

Whether the vision was an illusion or something else didn't matter, Ava decided, understanding it was time to return to The Cendryll, where she could wonder at the power of an artefact that twisted time.

"I don't think anyone's a favourite at the moment," Olin commented, pointing to Roan's adventure in the trading lane in Tallis & Crake ... the ceiling exploding as Roan span within a storm of shrapnel, protecting his face the best he could as he was dragged into position by an army of white insects. "Roan did brilliantly and so did you, Ava, but we all needed help in the end."

"I barely made it — again," Ava stated, glancing at the brass star in the palm of her hand.

"But you did," her dad added, blowing a flurry of Quij into existence, the luminous insects resting on Ava's shoulders: a touch of comfort for a girl struggling with a sense of inadequacy.

"Absolutely," Olin added, echoing Henry Blin's words. "Casper's faith in me was the help I needed. Jacob was there for Roan in the trading lane, and a girl lent a helping hand to you, Ava. Maybe faith's going to be the dividing line in the end: the difference between success and failure."

"Were you born this wise?" Roan joked, elbowing Olin to shift their attention from the floating parchment.

"An old soul my dad calls me."

"Well, old soul, how about teaching us how to sense things better? With a game, maybe."

"What game?"

"I don't know: hide and seek?"

"Really?" Ava queried, pulling a face. "We're not little kids."

"But we are struggling to keep up," Roan countered, "and Olin could be our second teacher. "If we can develop his sixth sense for the presence of things, it might give us an advantage. The Disira charm can take us to unfamiliar places in The Cendryll, and Olin can teach us how to sense our surroundings better."

"Which will help us to react quicker," Ava added.

"Right," Roan echoed. "If you don't mind, that is."

"I don't mind at all," Olin replied with a smile, his small

figure hidden within loose trousers and a baggy jumper: the secret weapon in Roan and Ava's return to winning ways.

"Only within the confines of The Cendryll, without waking anyone up," Ava's dad commented, looking on in amusement as the classmates enjoyed the luxury of staying up late. "I doubt a game of hide-and-seek is something I should be authorising at such a late hour, but I admire your determination."

The other students were indulging in similar games in various parts of The Cendryll, overseen by family members who understood the importance of childhood exploits. They were children, after all, needing the freedom to explore the S.P.M.A. beyond the confines of magical trials.

Henry Blin had craved the life his daughter was reaching for, dreaming of adventures in wild realms, but his wife had put a stop to this idea when the children were born, allowing him to exist in the Society in the day whilst the above-ground world took precedence in the evening.

Family duty came first for him, although this didn't stop Henry dreaming, delighted when Ava was chosen from a shortlist of children.

"Good idea to use the Velinis charm," Henry commented, pointing at Roan's figure on the floating parchment, hovering above them in the middle of the room.

"Thanks," Roan commented, reliving his adventure in the trading lane of Tallis & Crake.

Like Olin, Roan had discovered another slice of magic, revealing itself when he shattered the ceiling of the trading lane: a space formed of twisted beams that dripped a sweet residue onto his skin. The residue burnt on contact, but Roan knew how to mitigate this, taking out a vial of Srynx Serum to heal the pain.

When the treacle-like residue became almost impossible

to walk on, he used a flight charm to reach the twisted beams, jumping from one to the other as he followed a river of white light that ran across the floor ... light that eventually rested on the beam that spat splinters of wood in every direction ... the wooden beam protecting the prize he desired ... a golden pin that looked markedly unspectacular.

"So, what was it all about?" Ava asked her dad. "The midnight trial, I mean?"

Adjusting the belt on his green dressing gown, Henry Blin replied, "Something and nothing."

"Meaning ...?"

"Meaning it was just another test to assess your progress. As the days pass, the assessments will become more challenging: theoretical and physical."

"Like exams?" Olin queried, feeling confident of passing any knowledge-based test.

"Yes, Olin. There will be exams along the way. Memory is as important as bravery in the S.P.M.A. After all, there's a lot to remember."

"But the prizes were chosen for *us*," Roan prompted.

"Yes, to see if you could find them," Henry replied with a mischievous smile.

"*Obviously*," Olin replied, studying the glowing orb in her right hand. "Why make us hunt for something which could have just been given to us? It doesn't make sense. There's more to this than you're telling us, Mr Blin."

"*Dad*," Ava challenged, knowing when her father was hiding something from her.

"All I can say is that your prizes will test you," Henry added, moving towards the log fire, the flames leaving decorative patterns on the brickwork. "A test of your resolve when it matters most."

"To see if we'll make the grade," Roan commented,

wondering what power a golden pin could have.

"Indeed," Henry replied, watching the flames spin their elaborate patterns.

Deciding they'd had enough of mystery for one night, the friends studied the moving illustrations on their tongues, the magical sweets of Wimples offering a welcome delight and hilarity. All sweets from Wimples were laced with magic, the reason children travelled from all over the country to experience the wonder.

The illustrations left on the tongue couldn't be explained by above-ground adults, but the children needed no explanation, delighting in a moment of inexplicable joy. An angry professor appeared on Roan's tongue, wagging his finger in fury, whilst a train roamed around Ava's. Olin's offered a different image all together: a strange insect arching its back as it rested on the edge of his tongue.

Were the sweets a new arrival? Ava wondered. A bestseller children were scrambling for in the tiny shop on Leaning Lane? Something they'd missed since stepping into the wonderland of The Cendryll?

"What is it?" Roan asked, inching closer to Olin's diminutive figure.

"A Vanarix," Ava's dad replied.

"A what?"

"An insect you don't want to bump into."

"Why would the Society authorise illustrations of creatures on sweets?"

"They haven't," Henry replied.

"Then why did it appear on my tongue?" Olin asked, looking a little uneasy.

"Why indeed?" Henry Blin replied mischievously, sipping his hot chocolate to avoid eye contact with his daughter.

He knew why the insect had appeared, but was under strict orders to say nothing. It was a psychological test the students would soon face, revealing who would turn on a classmate considered to have been 'marked'. Olin was the most natural magician of the group, completing trials with ease and able to out think his classmates.

This, of course, led to a degree of jealousy in some, particularly Ethan and Katie who believed they were destined for greatness. It made sense, therefore, to use the spell on Olin, lacing one sweet with the insect's mark. All it took was an adult to be present, orchestrating things to ensure the sharpest magician in the pack selected the right sweet at the right time.

Ava's dad was the obvious candidate for this task, mainly because he often stayed up late with Ava, discussing her progress. The offer of a midnight feast, encouraging Ava to invite her closest classmates, was the next step. The only question remaining was who would turn on Olin first.

It wasn't something Henry wanted to dwell on, hoping his daughter wouldn't fall into this trap. Fear did strange things to people, though, meaning Jacob's class were in for a bumpy ride soon. Tonight was about fun, though, not wanting to dwell on what lay ahead.

"If you're going to test your skills, you'd better get a move on," Ava's dad suggested. "Also, I'll deny all knowledge if you land yourselves in trouble,"

Disappearing beyond The Cendryll would cause obvious problems, Henry knew, captors and malevs roaming the midnight streets, up to no good and always keen to take advantage of the meek. Sleeping soldiers protected the Society day and night, however, giving him comfort as his daughter and friends vanished, chasing a moment of innocence in a whirlwind of wonder.

11

SHIFTING TARGETS

With the midnight rendezvous over, attention returned to more traditional methods of teaching, namely the classroom based on the fifth-floor. Jacob had arrived early to prepare for the day, conscious of the weight of responsibility resting on his young shoulders. He knew more than he could say about last night's hunt, and the artefact each student had found.

The fact each one was a bovie — an artefact with complex magical properties — bothered him the most, largely because bovies had *unknown* powers. This was another decision made by The Orium Circle, the lawmakers deciding the simplest way of assessing each student's character was to offer them a magical mystery.

What The Fateful Eight would do with their powers was yet to be seen, leaving Jacob to explain the twist in the tale ... that they were being let loose to some degree. Geographical limitations remained — Society Square being the boundary they were forbidden to go beyond alone — but Jacob knew even this rule would blur in time, when the physical trials became more brutal and fear mixed with desperation.

His money was still on Katie to fall first, the girl so obsessed with winning. Power wouldn't serve Katie well, Jacob knew, standing beside the desk of blue light he'd formed courtesy of the Canvia charm. Ethan would struggle with the same predicament, the mixed-race boy blessed with a famous name.

The Lyell name was synonymous with power and authority, although each had been earned by the legendary Lyells in the S.P.M.A., including Weyen and Lyell and his deceased sister, Ina. Whether Ethan could find the right balance of humility and bravery was yet to be determined, Jacob knowing this to be the hardest test his students would face.

Power, after all, did strange things to the lucky few, testing moral principles and turning heads in the wrong direction. It affected children as much as any other age group, filtering through flaws and dreams until it rested in the deeper recesses of the human mind.

The Society members tasked with running magical faculties had proven themselves worthy, able to master this difficult balance, humble enough to see themselves as servants to a greater good.

"Who survives?" Jacob whispered as he flicked a coin into the air, the silver coin formed from the Vaspyl he'd taken out of his trouser pocket.

Dressed in his usual attire of jeans, untucked shirt and Society tie, the teacher tasked with guiding the lucky few caught the coin, studying the face forming on its surface ... of a boy marked with an equally famous name ... Tom Koll ... the pale, sullen boy burdened by an infamous uncle.

Time and time again, it was Tom's face that appeared on the coin, Jacob wondering if the boy's determination to atone for his uncle's mistakes made him the favourite.

"Who fails?" Jacob posed, throwing the silver coin into the air again, deciding to put it back in his pocket without looking at the result, understanding the dangers of tempting fate and meddling with time.

A Now-Then could return you to the past, but nothing could truly read the future, the silver coin showing the owner what they wanted to see. What Jacob *really* wanted to see was no face on the coin, when the question of 'Who fails' was asked, but he knew this was a fantasy he shouldn't be entertaining.

Some would fail and others would face danger, despite all the precautionary measures put in place. Power in the hands of the young was a danger in itself, Jacob knew, still uncomfortable with the decision to provide each student with a bovie.

"Their prizes will call to them," Ilina had suggested last night in The Illustrated Quarter. "Like certain stars are tempting you."

Jacob moved his hand along The Cathedral of Stars they walked within, two Society members who had found peace in each other's company. Not one to love easily, Ilina had trusted her instincts with Jacob — the young man whose gentle nature drew her in.

A few years younger, Ilina was searching for something else beyond faculty duty and evenings in Rebel's Rest. She had never tasted true danger nor the blizzard of war, knowing Jacob had experienced both. In moments of reflection, she wondered how the relationship would grow, accepting a life lived in different faculties made it challenging.

The Leverin offered a life of mercurial creation, infusing penchant stones with magical properties. It was fulfilling in some ways but wouldn't be forever, she knew, aware of the reclusive nature of the work in a magical faculty known for its industry.

The Cendryll buzzed with life, the luminous Quij decorating the faculty with beautiful light whilst Williynx used their beaks to assess powders used in charms — the majestic birds of Gilweean adding additional glamour to the faculty Jacob taught in.

If their relationship developed, they would have to address the question of co-habitation, the most likely solution running an above-ground establishment, Ilina having her eye on The Spinning Shoe. For now, evening walks in romantic locations would suffice, The Illustrated Quarter taking them to a glittering hallway of stars.

"What makes you think the stars are calling me?" Jacob had asked with a wry smile, knowing this was exactly what was going on, certain stars twinkling more brightly as his hand moved over them.

"You're restless," Ilina stated, studying the faint scars on Jacob's hand. "A teacher hiding his warrior instinct."

"That's more Guppy than me."

"Don't kid yourself, Jacob. You're not so different from your sister."

"Maybe."

"Definitely."

"And what about you?" Jacob prompted, turning to the girl who was slowly capturing his heart, striking in looks and regal in manner.

"I'm just enjoying the moment," Ilina replied, planting a kiss on Jacob's lips that lasted longer than anticipated, the power of love a unique type of magic no remedy could provide.

Jacob knew the prizes would call to the students, in various ways and at different times, but first they had to learn to master the power within them: the focus of today's lesson.

"How come I get a piece of thread and Leah gets a weapon weaved into her arm?" Katie moaned as the class arrived, appearing through portals of light.

"The golden thread obviously does something," Ethan offered, hoping to reassure his classmate who was burning with envy.

"Well, I didn't sign up for *knitting classes*," Katie countered, looking at her trouser pocket with disgust, the position of her Keepeasy where the golden thread was kept.

"If you want to swap it for a smoking pendant, be my guest," Ethan replied, getting a little annoyed with Katie's constant moaning.

While Ava, Roan and Olin were playing hide-and-seek to master the Disira charm, Ethan, Katie and Tom had locked themselves away in Heaven's Chamber, hoping this testing ground would reveal the hidden powers contained in their prizes.

Realising this wasn't the case, they negotiated the exploding staircases to reach the top of the training chamber, standing alongside one another as they surveyed a vague landscape. As the clouds brushed their faces, the three classmates had pondered their futures, frustrated that their prizes had revealed nothing despite hours of trying.

"When do we get to go *out there*?" Ethan had asked, pointing to the shooting light and vague outline of mountains in the distance.

"When it matters most," Tom replied with a degree of certainty, wondering what power lay in a brass chain.

"Well, I want to see it," Katie added, her anger increasing each time she studied the golden thread, hardly the prize she'd hoped for. "See all of it, including what lies beyond The Society Sphere."

"You know we can't do that," Ethan challenged.

"Do what?"

"Go beyond The Society Sphere."

"There're a lot of things we can't do, but that doesn't mean it's not going to happen."

"Leading to us getting kicked out," Tom added, echoing Ethan's point.

"Who said anything about *us*?" Katie queried, glancing at her classmates as if they were nuisances. "Whatever it takes to succeed, I'm going to do it even if that means bending a few rules."

"You push too hard sometimes," Ethan commented, patting his afro hair in a sign of boredom, "and it's likely to get you into trouble."

"Well, *mum* I know what it takes to win."

"It's not about winning, Katie; it's about *graduating*. The real victory comes afterwards, when we can roam anywhere we want: a life of magical living."

"You're leaving it up to chance and I'm not," Katie had concluded, running the golden thread through her fingers as she peered through the clouds, secretly planning her first visit beyond The Society Sphere. Also, there was the question of the spider appearing on Olin's tongue, something Katie would use to her advantage when the time came.

A LOUD CLAP FROM JACOB GOT THE GROUP'S ATTENTION, THEIR young teacher looking more upbeat than normal. Leah took the precaution of checking in on her teacher sometimes, knowing all about his romantic trip to The Illustrated Quarter last night.

Not quite stalking, Leah viewed it as understanding Jacob better: a young man with such an incredible story. The other girls knew Leah had a secret crush on their teacher, allowing her to indulge in a fantasy.

"I see you've all wrapped up as requested," Jacob began, sipping his Liqin from a silver mug. "We head off on a new journey this morning, and the temperatures are likely to be below freezing."

"To The Winter Quarter?" Ava queried, excited at the prospect of visiting a wonderland of snow.

"No, somewhere close by. Enemies will appear in many guises, so be careful who you trust as we proceed. Desks at the ready."

With an utterance of 'Canvia', the students created desks and chairs, forming two rows of four before perching on them. Talk of enemies got the classroom buzzing with intrigue, some more keen than others to discuss the subject. For Ethan and Katie, it was point they'd been waiting for, *finally* getting their teeth into true Society living.

Lessons had their place but knowledge alone wasn't going to keep the S.P.M.A. safe from harm, *action* was. Ava was less enthusiastic about the idea, wondering if talk of enemies was a ploy to draw out those with violent intentions: Katie at the front of this list.

"First of all, well done for locating your prizes. The next step is to understand what they can do."

"Ava already knows," Katie moaned, placing her elbows on the desk of light.

"Ava worked it out," Jacob countered, ignoring Katie's sullen tone, "and now it's your turn. Like all learning, development is the key and now you've mastered key elements of magic, it's time to extend your knowledge of The Society Sphere."

An excited look crossed the face of the class, drawing a smile from their teacher.

"It's also important to understand that your prizes are unstable."

"Meaning?" Tilly asked.

"Meaning their magical properties aren't clear."

"So, they could be good or bad?"

"Potentially."

"You've got to be kidding," Ethan piped up, swinging back on his chair of light. "You're trusting us with bovies? What if we mess up and blow something up ... or someone?"

"Then your time will be up."

"You want to see how the power affects us," Olin commented, still bemused by his orb of light. "To see if they tempt us into doing the wrong thing."

"Correct, Olin," Jacob added. "Ultimately, we can't have unstable witches and wizards amongst us, and your bovies will draw out any irrational thoughts. The more unstable they become, the harder you'll have to work to control them."

"So, we need to control it before it controls us?" Leah asked, studying the weave of silver on her right arm.

"Yes, Leah, then use it when the time's right."

"Which is?"

"When an enemy appears."

"Which could be anyone."

"Correct, but you've been given certain objects for a reason. Your job is to know how and when to activate them: the principle of subtle sorcery we all live by. If you're successful, you're learning will continue above ground where mistakes are critical. The part of The Society Sphere we're travelling allows for mistakes, so stick together and learn quickly. Ready?"

The class nodded as they stood to leave, Katie alone all of sudden as Ethan and Tom stepped away from her, joining forces with Leah. They'd sensed something at the top of Heaven's Chamber last night, something in Katie neither liked. The 'who said anything about us?' comment enough to distance themselves from her.

Friendship and trust would guide them through difficult times, when they didn't know the answer and were desperate for guidance, not classmates acting like enemies.

"And you're going dressed like that?" Tilly asked, glancing at Jacob's usual attire.

"I've got a coat somewhere," Jacob replied before throwing the silver mug into the air, stepping back as it morphed into a wardrobe ... the Vaspyl working its wonders.

As the silver wardrobe landed on the wood-panelled floor, Jacob knocked before entering, adding a little humour to the occasion. Seconds later, he reappeared with a coat, scarf and hat, clicking his fingers to send the wardrobe spinning into the air again, catching the silver coin in his right hand.

"Still my favourite artefact after all this time," he added, buttoning the fur-lined coat. "Handy and efficient."

"Couldn't we have used it to get where we're going?" Roan asked, still flummoxed by the gold pin he'd acquired last night, understanding little more than the fact it pierced his hand whenever he held it.

"Of course," Jacob replied, "but novelty has its place."

"So, how *are* we getting there?"

"Through the window," Jacob replied, tempted to flick

the silver coin before they left, but eventually deciding against it.

"Cool," Ethan added, gripping the smoking pendant. "At least this thing will keep me warm; it's like a mini fire in your hand."

"Well, get ready for a bit of theory," Jacob added, gesturing for the class to step towards the window, situated on the west wall.

A collective groan filled the room, the thought of a theory lesson generating whispers of frustration. Jacob's idea of theory was something else all together, though.

12

TELL TALE SIGNS

Transportation through the window was a simple matter of touch and timing, each student placing the hand decorated by their penchant on the window frame. The class waited patiently for the expected to happen, leaning back when the window frame stretched to the floor, the glass panes tinkling as they loosened in the wooden frame.

Ethan caught sight of an ice pyramid, wanting to touch the panes of glass but deciding this was unwise. Going against Jacob's instructions was a sure way to stand out as trouble, something Ethan wasn't keen on doing. Judging by Katie's plans to break Society protocol, she was going to be all the trouble Jacob could handle, Ethan thinking it best to play the role of committed classmate.

He wasn't going to do anything to jeopardise his chances of success, even if that meant distancing himself from Katie: the girl on a mission to prove something to herself.

"Grab on," Jacob instructed as the window fell outwards, pulling the students and their young teacher with it ... a window that turned into a sleigh as it expanded ... the panes of glass acting as rudders as they cut through the ice ... the ice pyramid Ethan glimpsed coming into full view now.

It was *blisteringly* cold, a strange wind blowing around them as they whizzed along the ice. As they raced along, Olin lost his grip on the makeshift sleigh, grabbing Roan's arm as they rose higher towards the tip of the pyramid.

"I'm going to fall!" Olin shouted, looking to Jacob for help.

"Then let go," Katie suggested, still fuming over her feeble prize.

It was sound advice, Olin decided, seeing no danger in releasing his grip ... the flight charm activated as he did ... but the propellor-like motion of the flower he created froze immediately ... leaving him helpless as the others whizzed along the walls, cutting their trajectory in the ice.

Sensing the danger her friend was in, Ava decided it was time to test the powers of the silver star. She wasn't going to leave a friend stranded and needed to prove herself equal to the others, having fallen behind in recent weeks. Releasing herself from the window, she uttered 'Comeuppance', taking the artefact out of her jeans' pocket.

'Exhibius' was the next command ... the spell required to split the star into five pieces ... each piece spinning near her face as she fell ... knocked off balance by the blistering wind that flooded the ice pyramid ... her next move proving to be her best yet.

With the wind blinding her temporarily, Ava watched as the splintered star spun around her forefinger: a weapon ready to be released on a friend in need. Today's lesson was about faith, she decided, remembering the way the splintered star had shown her a past moment, hoping her faith in herself would reap dividends.

She flung the star towards Olin's falling figure, watching

as it darted towards his small body, free falling towards a brutal ending. If she was wrong, Olin was seconds away from death, but she was sure of herself for the first time ... sure the silver star twisted time as it had in Senreiya.

It was an artefact Ava had never seen before, but one that had aligned itself to her, coming to the aid of a friend in a critical moment, framing Olin's body moments before he hit the ground. As it did, a sudden retraction began, lifting Olin out of danger and Ava towards a moment of self-realisation she wasn't sure was forthcoming.

For the first time, she felt at one with magic, sensing the magical properties of an alien artefact in her possession. Why this was the case didn't matter, Ava knew, smiling at the sight of Olin spinning towards her.

"That was close," Olin commented, struggling with the freezing temperatures that Ava barely noticed.

"My turn to help out," Ava replied, grabbing Olin's freezing hand.

"You're warm. Don't you feel the cold?"

Ava shook her head. "It must be this."

"The star of salvation," Olin joked, thankful it had come to his rescue. "Thanks for rescuing me."

"You've rescued me loads of time."

"Then we're even," Olin offered with a smile, the red coat and scarf protecting his face against the blistering wind.

As the sleigh ride came to an end, the window guiding the others towards Ava and Olin, the walls of the pyramid collapsed, leaving the group standing on a square of ice: a stage for the next phase of learning.

. . .

"So Ava's got a superpower," Roan commented with a smile, happy to see his friend recover some ground on her classmates.

"It just sort of happened," she replied, trying hard to play things down.

"How did you know how to activate it?" Tilly asked, slightly envious of Ava's new prize.

"I just guessed," Ava replied, aware of the hidden resentment of the others.

It was the first time she'd been ahead of the pack, the tall girl with slow reactions suddenly in tune with a new prize … a star that reversed time … time being the one thing you didn't meddle with. A Now-Then took you back to the past, but even that artefact was used rarely.

So, why had Ava been gifted with a star that twisted time? A test to see if she would fall under its spell, or a burden she had yet to realise? Either way, the envy of some classmates was evident, Ethan and Katie wondering why the girl with no particular gifts had been blessed with an obvious advantage.

"I can't feel my toes," Ethan commented as he shivered alongside Leah.

"You'll warm up soon," Jacob replied, turning his Vaspyl into an umbrella as he tapped the stage of ice. "

"Enjoying this morning's adventure so far?"

"It sounds like we're about to go on another one," Tom commented, his arms crossed across his thin, pale figure.

"A journey of discovery this time," Jacob explained, "working in groups of twos or threes, which is where the theory part of today's lesson comes in. The most important thing to remember about bovies is they're not aligned to you. They're not aligned to anything until their source of magic is uncovered."

"So, they could backfire on us?" Tom prompted.

"Possibly but unlikely, unless you ignore the warning signs."

"Which are?" Olin asked, conscious he'd already received a questionable sign on his tongue: a spider no one had mentioned since.

"Incessant hissing or buzzing," Jacob explained. "If this happens, create a steel box from your Vaspyl and place the object inside. Do *not* open the box until instructed."

"Secondly, bovies draw the attention of those seeking unique artefacts, which is where enemies come in. The people to look out for are those that hover too long ... study from a distance and appear without warning."

"Captors and malevs," Tilly commented, her freckled face suggesting she was troubled by something.

"And others of their kind," Jacob added. "Blackmarket rats who are skilled at gaining a stranger's trust."

"And we use our new weapons if an enemy appears?" Ethan queried, shivering alongside Tom.

"Yes, assuming you can activate them."

"A battle then."

"More of a puzzle," Jacob replied as he opened the umbrella.

"Sounds boring?" Katie added, her hopes of battling with captors and malevs dashed.

Jacob smiled as the first cracks appeared on the ice. "I doubt you'll find it boring. Remain alert and be prepared to read the signs — the most important part of today's venture. Finally, act on what you *sense* and not what you see."

"Not much to go on, is it?"

"It should be enough, assuming you've kept up with your homework," Jacob replied. "Society history has been part of your theory lessons, something you'll need to draw on to spot the signs."

Olin, Ava and Roan exchanged a glance, uneasy at the mention of homework. There were far better things to do than visit the Society library, including taking midnight trips to favourite locations, so if homework was necessary for this adventure they were *definitely* going to fail.

"So, we look out for shifty movements based on what we know and *feel*?" Ethan asked, keen to get clarity on the task at hand.

"Yes," Jacob concurred, moving to the periphery of the ice platform. "Peace comes at a price, Ethan, and there's no peace without prevention. The battles you're so desperate for will come later, assuming you can maintain peace first. The cracks of ice will lead you on, leaving me to observe from a distance, helping to avoid anyone getting killed or captured."

"Thanks," Katie replied with a sarcastic smile, keen to get on with things and move up the leaderboard. She didn't need friends to help her, staring at Ethan with a look of contempt.

At least they were finally getting to the juicy stuff, Katie thought, excited at the prospect of tracking questionable characters with new weapons. Today sounded like the first step towards a life of action, the element of danger triggering a surge of excitement in her.

She could finally step out of the safe confines of The Cendryll, moving freely between witches and wizards in unfamiliar terrain, precisely what she'd been hoping for. Training had its place but it wasn't magical living, Katie knew, tired of theoretical learning where no one got hurt or even injured.

Like Jacob said, peace came at a price and Katie was willing to pay whatever price was necessary to graduate, including putting herself in harm's way when the time came. Potential harm was on the agenda now as the ice cracked beneath their feet, creating slopes that sent them on their way, beginning a new hunt for unknown faces in unfamiliar spaces.

"We probably should have done our homework," Roan said as he, Ava and Olin worked as a trio, sliding towards an uncertain location, the slope extending as far as the eye could see.

"Lucky I've got a photographic memory," Olin joked, tapping his head with his fist. "There's genius in here."

"The genius that almost crashed to his death a few minutes ago," Ava countered with a friendly nudge.

"I needed a power nap."

"You need to pay attention," Roan added, his thin frame wrapped in a black coat and checked scarf.

"I'll snap into action when the time comes."

"Or get snapped in half," Ava teased, growing in confidence since her rescue mission.

To be the first to uncover her artefact's powers had lifted her spirits, knowing she had the power to reverse time. It wasn't something to be used lightly, she knew, although the fact she *could* do it was intoxicating, wondering when it would be needed in critical situations.

Like Katie, Ava sensed danger in the morning's adventure, happy she had new powers at her disposal. The reins were coming off as Jacob allowed them more freedom beyond confined spaces. All they had to do was prove themselves worthy — worthy of the investment made in them.

With Ethan breaking away from Katie for the first time, choosing to partner with Leah and Tom, Tilly was forced to pair up with a girl who feared losing above all else. Tilly's face said it all, the pinched expression signalling annoyance. Katie was becoming increasingly unpopular, her demanding personality rubbing the others up the wrong way.

"Something tells me they're going to fall out," Ava whispered as the first glimmer of light appeared ahead.

"In a bad way," Olin concurred, studying the orb of light in his right hand, "which is when the fun really begins."

13

LESSONS IN LOYALTY

As the ice slopes melted away, a new vision became apparent via shafts of glimmering light, stretching high above. Nothing could be seen beyond this, Ava reaching out to touch the curtain of light closest to her. According to Jacob, they were near The Society Sphere although there were no signs of snow, ruling out The Winter Quarter.

Jacob had said as much but Ava remained hopeful, drawn to the beauty of the realm of perpetual snow. There was no raucous sound either, suggesting they weren't in touching distance of The Singing Quarter, the question of where they were the first puzzle to solve.

"Be careful," Olin said as Ava stroked the curtain of light again. "It could be a trap."

"If it is, I'll use my star to reel us back to safety," Ava replied with a smile, her grey coat protecting her from the arctic temperature.

"The others have gone," Roan commented, stamping his feet to get some feeling back in them, "so I say we get a move on."

"Agreed," Ava replied, stepping into the shaft of light, becoming immersed in it the moment she did.

"Ava ..." came the muffled voice of her two friends.

"It's fine — come on," she replied, waiting for Olin and Roan to appear alongside her.

"It looks like a cathedral," Roan commented, staring up at the colossal structure they'd stepped into ... a spectacular vision made of glittering light that Jacob knew well: The Cathedral of Stars.

"Where do you think we are?" Olin asked, unbuttoning his black coat as the temperature rose suddenly.

"No idea," Ava replied, "but it's beautiful."

"A map of stars," Roan added, mildly awe-struck by the vision. "Now we just need to find a way out."

"I'd rather stay," Ava added, running her hand along the walls. "It's peaceful here."

"Staying won't get us any brownie points," Roan added, "so let's find a way out."

Knowing this was the only option they had, Ava kept pace with the others, making a mental note to return another time once she'd identified their location. Time was the deciding factor, after all, working against them whenever they were faced with another test.

Today's test was about discovery, realising the potential of their prizes as danger presented itself. Who the enemies would be was another puzzle, Roan finding it hard to believe Jacob was going to put them in real danger, but assumptions got you nowhere fast in the S.P.M.A. so none would be made.

"Look," Olin said, pointing to his right. "Tilly and Katie running from something."

"The signal to get out of here," Ava said as a sound reverberated around them.

Turning at the sudden noise, the trio activated defensive charms, taking no chances in unknown territory.

"I say wee use a Cympgus," Roan suggested, his right hand covered in flames of fire: the Smekelin charm at the ready.

"Agreed," Olin added, standing in a circle of protective light.

It was left to Ava to generate the portable Perium, uttering 'Whereabouts' as a ball of light appeared from her penchant bracelet, forming an archway seconds later. The ruby-coloured Perium shimmered unsteadily, suggesting it was at odds with the surrounding energy field.

"Let's go before that sound turns into something else," Ava said, grabbing Roan's arm as they stepped into darkness, appearing in a busy street moments later.

The street they'd stepped onto gave them no clues of their whereabouts, until they spotted the large illustrations on the walls of the buildings.

"The Illustrated Quarter," Olin said, smiling as a group of ageing wizards appeared through an image depicting a fountain of remedies: a spectacular vision in multi-colour the trio were keen to see.

Simple in principle and quaint in execution, The Illustrated Quarter drew witches and wizards who enjoyed strolling from one delight to another. After all, duty took its toll and not every Society member was drawn to the wonders of The Winter Quarter, or the manic nature of The Singing Quarter.

"Amazing," Roan commented, studying the multi-coloured fountain surging up the wall of the closest building, cascading down into teacups as Society members perched on the tiered seating areas, enjoying the wonder only magic could offer.

"Hilarious," Olin added, wondering if they'd have time to sample the delights of The Illustrated Quarter.

"I say we check it out," Ava suggested as they reached the crossroads.

As the wording on the signpost changed, the classmates caught a glimpse of another trio: Katie, Leah and Tom beating them to it as they stepped through the poster of a fountain of wonder.

"Do we follow them?" Olin asked.

"Jacob said we need to stay in our groups, so let's head somewhere else," Ava suggested, taking off her scarf as the sun rose above their new surroundings.

"I don't see any danger so let's look around," Roan added, sensing there was a trap ahead but unsure of what kind.

The current mystery was where the danger lay, he knew, enticed by the spectacles flickering into life on the grand buildings, each one stretching to an impossible length. Why not have some fun until the enemy appeared? he concluded, still uncertain of the powers hidden in the gold pin piercing his hand.

Perhaps today's adventure was a test of fear, Roan surmised, remembering the sight of Katie and Tilly running for cover in The Cathedral of Stars. Was it a real threat or an illusion ...? An illusion created by Jacob who was watching from a distance. Maybe he was much closer than they realised, pulling the strings from a comfortable position out of sight.

"What about there?" Olin suggested, pointing to a building decorated with an illustration of flying bicycles.

"Perfect," Ava replied, sharing Roan's belief that danger could be negotiated when it presented itself. Until then, it was time to have some fun in a realm of ever-changing wonder.

The flying bicycles rode of their own accord, moving along the ceilings and walls of the establishment they'd entered. A collection of single and double seaters, they offered a joyride for witches and wizards preferring simple pleasures. The scale of the space was the most striking thing, stretching for more than a mile in each direction.

It was a simple case of jumping on, the Affinyx charm used to attach yourself before you were whisked away, riding along the walls with your companion, romantic or otherwise.

"I say we jump on," Ava suggested, studying her reflection in the floor of mirrors.

"Agreed," Olin replied, content to be in a space where age wasn't frowned upon.

A few Society elders offered gestures of welcome whilst others merely went about their business, keen to get a break from more pressing matters, saddling up and cycling to their heart's content. It was a simple pleasure, Olin thought, but a welcome one.

After all, they'd spent their induction cooped up in a small classroom, learning how to activate dynamic charms before things intensified in Heaven's Chamber. If more of their lessons were like this, it was going to be a *wild ride*.

"Brilliant!" Roan exclaimed as they climbed the walls on their bicycles, wondering what could possibly go wrong in a morning free of mystery and mayhem.

While Ava, Roan and Olin went on a joyride, Tilly and Katie were taking cover in a less spectacular place, some distance from the figure they'd encountered. Whoever the figure was, they had thrown them into a panic, mainly because of the way they'd appeared *out* of the stars, like a zombie coming alive to capture its prey.

Tilly sensed there was more to this than met the eye, unconvinced their teacher would put them in genuine danger so early in their training, but they *had* seen something ... something ethereal and aware of their presence ... moving towards them at lightning speed.

Deciding safety was the best form of attack, the girls took solace in the first space they'd stumbled upon, having no idea how Periums worked in The Illustrated Quarter until they were hiding behind a building, sensing they were being followed.

When an enormous illustration appeared on the wall they had initially panicked, thinking it was another trap, until a whispered voice resonated on the other side of the wall, uttering the words "Quickly, before it's too late."

Whilst understanding the danger of accepting a stranger's offer, they also felt the need to get out of sight, shaken by the glimmering enemy who'd been within striking distance of them. Had it attacked, they would have been easy prey, too slow to activate a defensive charm or consider the secrets of their new artefacts: prizes with powers they would come to rely on.

It was a split-second decision they knew might cost them dearly, but one they felt compelled to make, stepping through the illustrated building into the company of a strange saviour, and an even stranger place.

The young woman was elegantly dressed, her disfigured face hypnotising Tilly and Katie. Engaging and friendly, she lifted her arms in welcome as if she was addressing long-lost friends.

Her surroundings were equally elegant, lamps floating in the air of various colours ... thousands of them rising in the air like kites. Unlike the locations their classmates had discovered, there was no burst of activity in this space, just the stranger for company.

"Doubt does damage over time," their disfigured lady stated, encouraging them to step closer. "It can be the difference between life and death."

"Who are you?" Katie asked, unskilled in the art of decorum.

"A guide."

"Or an enemy."

"Young Katie Follygrin, ever the aggressor," the young woman added, offering a forced smile as she did. "You should be thanking me for rescuing you."

"From what?" Tilly prompted.

"Certain failure."

"So, what was it?"

"A mirage that you fell for, meaning you have to make up lost ground now. Luckily, you've stumbled upon the right place. While your friends are enjoying the delights of The Illustrated Quarter, you have an opportunity to regroup."

"How?"

"By listening and learning," the stranger replied.

"Who are you?" Katie asked asking, deciding no listening *or* learning was going to happen until some trust was gained.

"An insignificant onlooker, tasked with helping you unlock hidden powers."

A comment that made the girls step back, sensing they may have fallen into a trap after all.

"Yes, I know about the prizes you've discovered, and your need to uncover their secrets. Every Society member knows so hold on to your rising suspicions. Everything you do is observed, so everyone you meet already knows you."

"Which doesn't help us to distinguish between the good and bad," Katie added, relieved the golden thread was tucked away in her Keepeasy.

"A hard distinction to make since we're all good and bad, Katie Follygrin. Take you, for example — the girl who stands at the pinnacle of Heaven's Chamber, fighting the urge to break Society protocol. You've dismissed offers of friendship along the way, making it clear you're more an enemy than an ally: your interpretation of what it means to be successful."

"I didn't mean I *was* an enemy," Katie protested, aware of Tilly stepping away from her. "I just meant ..."

"You just meant you'll do anything to win," Tilly interjected, feeling the glass baton come to life in her hand: the prize she'd discovered in Cribbe & Corrow.

"We all want to win," Katie countered.

"But at what cost?" the disfigured girl replied, studying her guest with a growing intensity.

"There doesn't have to be a cost," Katie added, aware she was losing the trust and respect of her classmates.

"There's always a cost," Tilly stated, the most studious of the group who'd read up on the last two battles. "This will stop being a game pretty soon, Katie, which is the reason we've got these *things* ... bovies we have to charm into action before it's too late."

"I never wanted this to be a game," Katie said, angry she'd shown weakness earlier. "I *want* it to get more dangerous so we can prove ourselves."

"Which is what you need to do now," the stranger interjected, pointing at the lamps floating above them, "heading back into the open and facing the next threat you see."

"And the lamps will take us there?" Tilly asked, studying the gold flecks spinning in her glass artefact.

"They will take you *somewhere*, Tilly Flint ... somewhere that will present a test."

"Meaning we have to trust you," Katie stated, just before the lamps went out and they were plunged into darkness.

"I *KNEW* IT," KATIE HISSED, UTTERING 'SPINTZ' TO ILLUMINATE their surroundings. "Now what?"

"We work our way out of here," Tilly replied, taking a vial of clear remedy from her pocket. "Here," she said, offering Katie the magical eyedrops known as Crilliun. "Just in case there's competing magic at play."

"Why would there be?"

"Because we've just been *had*, Katie, and now we've made *two* mistakes in the space of ten minutes. We gave into our fear, the very thing we weren't supposed to do. If we can't even *sense* the enemy, what chance do we have of defending ourselves against them?"

"Who said she was an enemy?"

"Well, she's *gone* and we're still here: *alone*."

"So, we just use a Cympgus to get us out of here," Katie suggested, brushing her blonde hair behind her ears.

"That's too easy. Jacob's sent us here to prove ourselves in some way, and we've failed spectacularly so far."

"Well, if you've got a *better idea*."

"We follow her guidance, finding a way to turn the lamps back on," Tilly suggested, increasingly annoyed with her classmates whining.

"*What?* You *must* be joking. We don't even *know where we are,* and you want to trust a nutter who's abandoned us."

"I thought you were the tough one."

"I *am.*"

"So grin and bear it. *I'm* using the lamps to get out of here; you can do what you want. *Fear* is the real enemy, Katie, the point you're missing."

"How do you mean?"

"There's no enemy out here. No bogey man and no evil witch or wizard. We're *kids* on trial with our every move being watched, like the lady said whoever she was. This all feels staged in a way, and it wouldn't surprise me if Jacob's looking on and laughing right now. We panicked at the first thing we saw, then fell into the first trap laid for us — not ideal candidates, are we?"

"So, we fix it," Katie replied, losing her petulant tone as she sensed Tilly was right: the girl with determination to match her intellect, still harbouring mixed feelings of the opportunity afforded to her.

Of all the students chasing a dream, Tilly was the least enraptured with the world of magic she'd discovered. This was partly due to the pressure her parents had placed on her, arguing that it would do wonders for the family name. Tilly had wondered why status and reputation was so important to her parents, spending more-and-more time in the Society library, hoping to come across stains on the family name.

A spectacular betrayal or a relative under suspicion, she'd surmised, but instead she'd learnt nothing more than dull duty, the reason her parents had grasped at the offer of glory. A sudden sensation drew her out of her reverie, glancing at the baton-shaped glass object in her hand ... the bovie she had no ability to unlock ... or so she thought.

She'd tried obvious spells such as 'Exhibius' and 'Magneia', hoping the artefact would reveal its powers, but standing stranded with a sense of duty weighing on her, she tried the most logical charm she knew, uttering 'Affinyx' in the hope that *alignment* was the key to activating the power her prize contained.

"What the *hell* ..." Katie commented as flecks of gold were released from the glass artefact, forming a mask that hung in the air ... the face of the figure who'd appeared zombie-like in The Cathedral of Stars.

The mask spun in mid-air, turning to offer a glimpse of the source of their fear.

"Do you recognise him?" Katie asked, careful not to make contact with the mask of gold dust.

"Nope."

"Well, at least it proves one thing."

"What's that?"

"That you're right about the enemy being our fear. *That's* the enemy staring back at us, the thing that made us run for cover, meaning the young woman was helping us after all."

"Maybe," Tilly offered, studying the gel-like substance in the palm of her hand, where the glass structure of the artefact had been.

"*Definitely*. The question is, what do we do now?"

"Follow it," Tilly suggested, determination written all over her freckled-face.

"Without fear," Katie replied with a smile, wondering if she'd found a friend amongst her classmates after all.

With the bovie releasing its secret, the only thing left to do was experience its unique sorcery, Tilly leading the way as the mask of gold dust retreated from them. Trusting her instincts, she rubbed the gel-like substance on her face, ensuring there was enough left for Katie before taking her classmate's hand. For the first time, Katie didn't question or challenge, realising that faith was likely to get her further than fury.

"Well, here goes nothing," Tilly said as the mask reversed its momentum, moving closer to the girls until it attached itself to Tilly's face, sucking the friends through a Perium of a different kind.

Soon, she would learn that the bovie in her possession was an Axiel: part Perium, part surveillance device. Unlike Follygrins and Panorilums, it could detect enemies in hiding, rendering invisibility charms useless. Once the subject had shown its face, it was imprinted in the flecks of gold, swimming in the glass baton until the time came to meet danger head on.

14

THE ILLUSTRATED QUARTER

As Tilly and Katie returned to face their fear, Leah, Ethan and Tom enjoyed the splendour of a fountain of remedies. Unlike anything they'd seen before, a singular fountain of colour dominated the space, surging up towards a glass ceiling flecked with sprinkles of the various remedies.

Leah spied familiar colours in the fountain — purple, green and orange — suggesting Jysyn Juice, Fillywiss and Srynx Serum were woven into its fabric. Surrounding the spectacular fountain was a tiered seating area, each level rising and falling to accentuate the sense of floating beneath a waterfall.

It was just the thing to take the trio's mind off potential enemies, no sign of which had appeared so far. Smiling at the multi-coloured brew in their teacups, the classmates sat on the highest tier of seating, looking down at the glass floor marked with splashes of colourful liquid.

It was a popular place, crowded with Society folk who entered through the north wall, the interior of the wall offering no such magical illusion. There was no need for enticement once you were inside, the surging fountain tempting the most cynical magician towards it, returning them to memories of innocent wonder.

"I could stay up here all day," Ethan said, swinging his legs as multi-coloured liquid splashed down, decorating his clothes as it re-filled his cup.

"Me too," Leah concurred, thankful for a break from their intense lessons.

Never one to moan, Leah was secretly missing aspects of the above-ground world, the fairground attraction of the fountain of remedies a memory of its beauty and simplicity. It wasn't that she wanted to return to more mundane living, just that she wanted some sense of balance to return, the thought of darting from one realm to another without pause giving her second thoughts.

As stunning as the S.P.M.A. was, it demanded *a lot*. Leah wanted to be certain she was willing to sacrifice simple pleasures before committing to a mercurial existence. Her parents were bemused at her doubts, representing the seventh generation of Creswells in the Society, but they also wanted their daughter to be happy, studying her exploits from a popular above-ground establishment: Gulliner's gift shop.

The bizarre array of gifts had always intrigued Leah: a Sensiril that chimed the most fractious child into slumber, and snow globes depicting *very realistic* representations of mythical lands. At least, this was the impression above-ground folk left with, having no idea of the wonders of The Winter Quarter.

In the end, she felt she could live with whatever decision she made. For now, at least, she was committed to the experience, keen to put her training to the test. Laughing as her black hair lifted as they rose again, Leah opened her mouth to gulp the mixture of remedies, blinking as a fizzing sensation ran through her.

"Maybe the fountain's the enemy," Tom said as their seating area lifted higher, tilting as it did. "About to crush us in its grip."

"It's about to do *something*," Ethan replied, suddenly unsure of the surreal ride, grabbing onto his wooden seat as they were immersed in the powerful fountain.

Overwhelmed by a sudden suffocating sensation, the trio were catapulted into the flood, tumbling head over heels as they collided into one another, enveloped in a kaleidoscope of wonder.

"So far so good," Jacob said, standing alongside three familiar faces: Ilina, Jalem and Harvey.

"How did I do?" Harvey asked, excited to be involved in practical magic.

"Splendid," Jacob replied with a smile, loosening the Society tie he grudgingly wore.

The young quartet stood in The Cathedral of Stars, aware of the layered nature of its boundaries. Forming a star constellation provided access into its deeper recesses, a romantic touch offering couples a little private time. Romance wasn't on the agenda this morning, but rather the study of progress — Ilina, Harvey and Jalem offering a helping hand.

Jacob had explained the nature of the morning's lesson, testing the student's ability to deal with their fears, the concept of an enemy enough to trigger their subconscious into action. Whatever fears they harboured would manifest, he knew, whether this was a fear of failure or something else.

Ilina's job was to disguise herself with a disfigurement charm, appearing when Tilly and Katie had lost their way, while Harvey enacted the role of ghost to trigger the girl's fear. So far so good, as Jacob had stated, leaving Jalem to enact the role of villain when Ethan, Leah and Tom were spat out of the fountain.

The *real fun* would begin then, Jacob's companions ready to draw the students into a fire fight at close quarters. Nothing too serious, of course, but enough to see who could react in time, and who ran for cover. It was Ilina's idea to use them as bait, keen to escape safer sanctuaries. It might also allow her to spend more time with Jacob, learning more about the active world of magic he lived in.

"So, remember," Jacob said, stepping onto the constellation of stars beneath his feet, "keep your identity hidden and draw them in, giving them time to enact their defences."

"What if they strike first?" Harvey asked, his reddening face suggesting he was having second thoughts.

"Then you'd better run for cover," Jacob offered with a smile, spinning on the next star he stepped on, pretending he was on a dance floor.

"You're enjoying this," Jalem stated, his tall figure towering over Harvey's.

"I am," Jacob replied, spinning again. "It's good to see you all doing some *real work*."

"Cataloguing charms is real work."

"Boring though."

"Well, it beats getting killed," Harvey added, deciding to break out into his own dance move.

"Says who?" Jacob countered with a smile. "Wait until you experience the thrill of battle, then you'll understand."

"Ready when you are," Ilina stated, taking Jacob's hand as they waltzed across the constellation of stars.

"They're getting into position," Jacob said, studying the floor as he waltzed, a simple way of tracking the students' progress. "Remember, creative charms only. I doubt you want a killing on your conscience."

"I feel sick," Harvey claimed, holding his excessive belly.

"You feel scared," Jalem teased, grabbing his friend's hand and swinging him into a waltz of their own.

"I can't feel my feet," Harvey moaned, entering a state of panic.

"Just swing your hips," Jalem suggested, spinning his friend until he'd proven his point ... fear was at the root of Harvey's panic attack ... the very thing they were tasked with drawing out of The Fateful Eight.

"Feel better now?" Ilina asked with a touch of sarcasm, happy to be close to Jacob again.

"Not really," Harvey replied, bent double at the thought of engaging in battle. "I'm worried I'm going to panic and electrocute someone."

"Probably yourself," Jalem joked, drawing a laugh from the others.

"Just stay calm, Harvey," Jacob instructed, ending his waltz to reassure his friend. "It's what you've wanted for months: a taste of action."

"But now it's here ..."

"You're nervous," Jacob interjected, "which is normal, but hold on to the *fun* of it. No one's going to get hurt — not today at least — so enjoy the experience."

"And if I *do* electrocute someone, or worse?"

"You'll have Casper Renn to deal with."

As a look of fear crossed Harvey's red face, the others burst into laughter, making him realise they were teasing him again ... the overweight boy who knew nothing of magic until eighteen months ago ... still spinning at the thought of being accepted into a world like no other.

"*There*," Tilly whispered, reappearing in The Cathedral of stars with Katie. "He's one of Jacob's friends."

They were some distance from Jacob and his friends, finding themselves in a pocket of space framed by fragments of light. Couples appeared out of other private spaces, looking a little dishevelled as they caught sight of Tilly and Katie.

"Looks like we've stumbled across Lovers' Lane," Katie commented, smiling at the sight of the girl adjusting her blouse.

"Might come in handy at some point," Tilly replied with a smile, keeping secret crushes close to her heart.

The time for love and longing would come, she knew, but first she had to make it out of this adventure in one piece, either established in the S.P.M.A. or returning above ground.

The Axiel had worked its wonders, the mask formed from the flecks of gold transporting them back to the place where fear took hold.

"I knew it was staged," Tilly added, her red hair falling over her green coat. "The enemy's the thing we fear, not a real enemy so to speak."

"How can you be so sure?" Katie asked, realising the benefits of friendship.

"He's right there," Tilly stated, pointing at the figure of Harvey ... moments before he vanished within a curtain of protection.

"About things in general, I mean," Katie elaborated. "You sensed this was staged straight away."

"It just seemed logical."

"Can I borrow some of that logic?" Katie replied with a smile, coming to terms with the limitations of arrogance. Humility was going to get her further, she understood, starting with an admission of her insecurities.

"Everything's harder than I thought it would be," she continued, retying her blonde hair into a bob. "I'm used to winning ... well, I *was* used to winning ... which is why I've found losing so hard."

"No one's losing, Katie," Tilly replied in a reassuring tone. "We're in this together. The more we work together, the better chance we've got of graduating."

"Understood," Katie replied. "So, we surprise him, whoever he is?"

"Yep," Tilly replied as Jacob vanished from sight, along with the two remaining companions. "Then we have some fun."

Fun wasn't the way to describe a journey through a fountain of colour, Ethan, Leah and Tom catapulted onto a well-polished floor. It was a comical sight, the trio soaked to the skin, trudging towards an ill-fitting doorframe. No one else seemed concerned with their condition, the classmates' shoes squelching across the floor.

"Well, we're in no shape to face an enemy," Tom quipped, flicking his head to rid himself of some sweet residue.

"We need to find somewhere to dry off," Ethan

suggested, annoyed at the state of his normally immaculate afro. "Ask someone, maybe, or just follow the crowd."

"Follow the crowd," Leah and Tom replied in unison, deciding not to trust their instincts in a realm where the quaintest thing could turn on you.

The doorway led them back to the space they'd started in, the fountain of remedies not holding the same attraction this time.

"It *is* like a fairground ride," Leah stated, feeling her clothes sticking to her skin. "You jump on, get thrown about and jump off."

"Once is enough for me," Ethan replied, deciding to take out the smoking pendant: his prize for completing last night's quest.

"Don't hold it out for everyone to see," Tom suggested, uneasy whenever coming across mysterious objects with strange powers. "You never know who's watching."

"Maybe that's the point," Ethan added, "making sure people *do* see it, drawing the enemy out of hiding."

"An enemy who might know what your bovie does, turning it on you."

"I'm *twelve*," Ethan replied with a disgruntled look, "and we're surrounding by Society elders. I say we use our bovies to tempt our targets, giving us a chance to explore more of The Illustrated Quarter afterwards.

"We'll let you be the guinea pig," Tom stated, not wanting to rely on the artefact he couldn't activate, morphing steel remaining the go-to object of choice.

"Fair enough," Ethan replied, throwing the smoking pendant in the air, drawing a reaction from a few Society stragglers who hovered in the recesses of the room.

"*There*," Leah said, pointing to their left. "He just moved, vanishing from one pillar to another."

Ethan closed in on the person of interest, gripping the pendant as white smoke began to pour out of it. "Looks like we've got company, after all," he said, wondering if he'd drawn something other than curiosity towards them.

THE LESSON IN THE ART OF ALCHEMY BEGAN WHEN EVERYONE was in play, Jacob moving to a different part of The Cathedral of Stars to judge proceedings. With Tilly uncovering the powers of her prize, things were going to get interesting for Harvey: the friend so keen to experience the thrill of battle.

This was a battle of a different kind, Jacob pitching his students against his friends in the knowledge no harm could be done, which wasn't to say it wouldn't be eventful. Like Ilina, Jalem had used a mixture of remedies to disfigure his face, ensuring he wouldn't be recognised by the trio he was closing in on.

Ilina didn't need her disguise this time, entering the realm of flying bicycles to make her mark. She spotted Ava, Roan and Olin gliding along the walls and ceiling, paying no attention to the crowd below: a perfect wall of noise to hide her movements.

Her job was simple, to cause chaos amongst the crowd, releasing doveflies from her Zombul. Jacob had convinced Ilina this would work, explaining that most Society members had never seen a creature in the flesh, terrified of their name let alone their presence.

The white insects multiplied and swarmed, directed by Ilina's Zombul as she pointed it at her target: the young trio peddling to escape an army of trouble heading their way.

15

THE ART OF ALCHEMY

With Harvey doing his best to remain illusive, Tilly and Katie closed in, pretending to be unaware of his exact position. The Axiam told them this, of course, the baton-shaped glass object releasing a gold mask, transporting the owner to their the target.

Unaware of the bovies each student had in their possession, Harvey struggled with rising anxiety as a flash of light whipped past him ... then another until the light stretched and multiplied ... moving towards him with menace. Struggling to contain his fear, Harvey activated the Disira charm to shift positions in The Cathedral of Stars, belching as the two girls pivoted with his rhythm.

How could they know his position ...? Was it a trick to force a false move from him or part of the force field of light surrounding him ... fibres of energy spiking as they tried to pin him into position. He moved again, this time through a Cympgus, easing into another private corner of the glittering space ... and again the girls turned to face him .... a clear sign they had the upper hand.

"Well, here goes nothing," Harvey whispered.

Taking a deep breath, he stepped out from his cover, ready to engage in the morning's 'get together', as Jacob liked to put it.

"Looks like you're winning now," Tilly said to Katie, nodding at the golden thread that was laced between her fingers, no spell uttered to activate it.

Instead, a feeling caused the thread to burst into life … a sense of purpose not linked to punishment or pain, but preservation … the fundamental essence of all things in the S.P.M.A. The aim was to preserve their place in the magical universe, until the time came when they would reach the necessary heights.

"Just surviving at the moment, which is good enough for me," Katie replied with a smile, moving in synchrony with Tilly as the two girls met Harvey's sudden strike head on … a burst of fire that swept along the floor … rising towards them in a wall of resistance.

This was easily contained by a flood of water, released by Tilly's utterance of 'Levenan', the water colliding with the flames and extinguishing the threat. Streaks of light and energy came next, Harvey trying the Promesiun charm this time, but Katie was equal to this, pivoting to release a rapid-fire attack that sent Harvey scuttling for cover … her golden thread retracting before it released a spray of ammunition … bullet-like in its ferocity.

With preservation being understood by all, no charm touched the boundaries of The Cathedral of Stars, the glittering stage offering a beautiful backdrop to a delicate dance. After all, the aim wasn't to injure or maim but to test, leaving Jacob to get a deeper insight into the character of his students before important decisions were made.

"So far, so good," Jacob whispered, more concerned for Harvey's safety than anyone else's. His friend panicked easily, over excitable and over weight none of which was likely to help as the morning duel intensified. "Touch and timing, Harvey," Jacob added as Tilly's wall of water became a collapsing tower of ice, causing Harvey to yell in fear as an avalanche descended onto him.

Touch and timing weren't gifts Harvey had, the reason he'd chosen a quiet existence in The Feleecian: the faculty for remedies. Also, no remedy would help him now, the collapsing ice tower threatening to crush the life out of him until Katie came to his rescue.

She weaved the golden thread through her fingers to create a blanket of protection over Harvey, the ice absorbed by Katie's mercurial manoeuvre as Harvey let out a scream of terror.

"That was close," Harvey offered as he was helped to his feet by Katie and Tilly. "I thought you were going to kill me for a second."

"I thought about it," Katie replied, bursting into laughter at the look of horror on Harvey's face.

Gasping for breath and pouring with sweat, his rotund figure wasn't made for battle, Jacob stifling his own laughter as he stepped into view. "Nice work, Harvey. You really had them on the run for a while."

"Very funny," Harvey replied, desperate to return to Rebel's Rest where he could regale his friends with his near-death experience.

"How did we do?" Tilly asked, knowing Katie wanted to.

"You played a perfect hand," Jacob offered with a smile of pride. "Working out your bovies at the ideal moment."

"And the others?" Katie asked, a look of genuine concern replacing a competitive scowl.

"About to engage in their own dance," Jacob added,

pointing a hand at the east wall of The Cathedral of Stars, uttering 'Exhibius' as he did.

As the stars formed into familiar shapes, Katie and Tilly stepped closer, moving their attention between the dividing line Jacob had created on the wall, offering separate visions of spectacular spaces where delicate dances were about to begin.

"That's the lady we saw earlier," Tilly stated, tying her red hair back as she pointed at Ilina's figure. "What's she releasing from her hands?"

"Doveflies" Jacob replied. "Harmless and elegant."

"They don't look harmless," Harvey replied, still recovering from his near-death experience.

"They string you up and lift you to an uncomfortable height, mildly strangling you in the process," Jacob explained without a trace of concern.

"Strangling?" Katie queried. "Hardly sounds harmless to me."

"It's more of a tickling sensation," Jacob added, offering Harvey a vial of yellow liquid: Liqin for the nerves. "Drink this before you pass out," he said as he handed Harvey the vial — his friend thankful for a dose of remedy to calm his nerves.

"Here we go," Jacob added as Ilina's army of white insects dragged Ava, Roan and Olin off their flying bicycles ... just as Jalem turned the fountain of remedies into a weaving weapon, directed at Ethan, Leah and Tom's stunned figures.

"*Now what?*" Ethan asked as his smoking pendant snapped open, revealing a face he didn't recognise.

"Hide!" Leah shouted before yelling 'VERUM VERAS' ... the trio taking the precaution of activating a blanket of protection.

With the fountain of remedies twisting like a tornado to the delight of onlooking witches and wizards, the classmates rose higher to avoid its lashing motion. The Verum Veras charm hid them from view, but nothing else. It offered no physical protection, meaning they needed to come up with a battle plan quickly.

"Doesn't that thing *do anything*?" Tom said, gesturing to the weave of steel decorating Leah's right arm.

"About as much as your brass chain," Leah replied with a touch of sarcasm, secretly frustrated she hadn't unlocked her bovie's powers.

"Well, now would be a good time for *one of us* to crack the code," Ethan added as the twisting tornado of remedies touched their heels, dragging them back into its crushing force field. "As in *right now*!" he shouted as they tumbled into trouble, Tom the one to act first, whipping the brass chain over his head in a sudden moment of clarity.

As the chain picked up speed, growing in length as it did, Tom regained an upright position, understanding what needed to be done in a crystal-clear vision. Countering the tornado of remedies required a competing structure ... one with the strength to hold firm within an erratic force field. Tom envisioned just the thing ... a triangular frame that ran to the bottom of the fountain ... like the shell of an elevator protecting them from external forces.

It was the only idea they currently had, Ethan and Leah getting sucked into the vortex again, leaving Tom to act quickly, shouting 'Bildin' as he whipped his vision into life, holding firm as the first layer was built around his friends' figures, allowing them to grab onto the brass frame.

"Stay on the *inside!*" Tom shouted as he continued his construction, learning the art of alchemy in an instinctive moment.

"What?" Ethan called back, blasted by another splash of colour.

"The *inside*," Tom repeated, pointing to the brass chain dangling down.

The Bildin charm allowed you to create anything imaginable, formed of light and energy, but a brass bovie took things to another level. Entire physical structures could be built, suggesting it was an artefact designed for surveillance, protection and escape.

The Disira charm worked wonders when you had control, not so good when you were tumbling into a vortex of pain. The brass chain, whatever it was, acted as an alternative escape measure, Tom whipping layer after layer into life until it was complete ... grabbing onto the brass chain that hung in the middle ... ready to face the young man who had chosen carnage as the morning's entertainment.

With the erratic fountain whipping out in all directions, causing amused onlookers to take cover around the permitter of the space, the classmates found their footing as multi-coloured liquid decorated the walls and ceiling ... as if the surging vortex was seeking an escape route.

Now it was time to test themselves against the stranger who stood opposite, using a Fora charm to keep the chaos at bay. Activating the same charm, the young trio stood under a blanket of light, the surrounding carnage muted by a spell designed to halt propelling shrapnel.

With the crowd of onlookers taking cover within Velinis charms, a delicate decoration lined the space, suggesting a sea a calm in contrast to the mayhem whipping around them. It was clear the young man wasn't an enemy but a test, evident in the stationary position of the Society crowds, enjoying the morning spectacle.

"Now what?" Ethan asked as the classmates stayed close together.

"Wait for him to strike," Leah suggested, suddenly confident on a very public stage. Her dark hair lifted as she uttered 'Promesiun', a multi-coloured surge of light surrounding the weave of silver, attached to her right arm.

"Is it me or does he look friendly?" Tom asked, deciding a Vaspyl was the best line of defence.

"*That* doesn't look friendly," Ethan countered, ducking as a familiar sight exploded into the air ... vampiric birds storming towards them.

"VELINIS!" the young trio uttered in unison, whipping their arms above their heads to generate bubbles of protection.

They knew this trick, having witnessed it in their lessons a few days ago. The young man acting as the enemy was using a Zombul — a silver artefact decorated with holes on the top. It was an ideal tool for training, releasing creatures under the user's control.

Now it was time to do more than hide, Tom knew, keeping his brass chain in his right hand, more aligned to its powers now. How it could counter an Ameedis attack was uncertain, but as the smoking pendant hovered above Ethan's hand, Tom spied a solution.

"If Leah can stun them, I think I know how to neutralise the vampire birds."

"How?" Leah asked, struggling with the pain piercing her right shoulder.

"With that?" Tom replied, nodding at Ethan's smoking penchant.

As the muted sound of the Ameedis rang in their ears, Tom elaborated.

"We know what my brass chain can do, so let's put your bovies to the test: the real point of this 'remedies for enemies' lesson."

"So, you think you know what they do?" Leah prompted.

With a nod, Tom added, "I think your weave of silver swarms the enemy, and Ethan's traps it."

"So they work together?" Ethan asked, studying the smoking pendant as the vampire birds darted between the roaring fountain of remedies, attempting to penetrate their shield of protective light.

"I think they all work together," Tom added. "All eight of them, but I can't explain why."

"Well, let's put it to the test," Leah suggested, grimacing as she lifted her right arm. "It's getting harder to move my arm so be quick, Ethan," she added, closing her eyes as the weave of silver drew blood ... blood that poured down her arm and along her neck.

"That's not good," Ethan commented, losing concentration at the wrong moment ... just as the avalanche of remedies buckled their shield of protective light.

"*Focus*," Tom commanded, clicking his fingers to get Ethan's attention. "When Leah releases whatever's in that weave of silver, throw the smoking penchant in the direction of the vampire birds."

Ethan nodded, annoyed he'd lost concentration again, a flaw he couldn't iron out.

"If they break through, I'm out of here," Leah said as she screamed her intent, opening her right hand to release a blistering web of light ... light that stunned the Ameedis on impact ... causing the vampiric enemy to float in mid air.

"*Now!*" Leah instructed, nodding for Ethan to throw his

smoking artefact towards the stranded enemy, uttering something indecipherable as he did.

There were easier ways to obliterate an enemy, he knew, but that wasn't the point of the morning's adventure ... the art of alchemy was ... the skill of aligning yourself to the weapon at hand in critical moments. Tilly and Katie had managed it, and now it was the turn of the second group, faced with a blizzard of venom courtesy of a stranger's touch.

As Ethan's pendant rose in the air, it opened, revealing no secrets inside other than a cracked mirror.

"Well, there goes your theory," Ethan commented, a familiar sinking feeling in the pit of his stomach forming, symbolic of another failed attempt at mercurial movements.

"Not quite," Tom replied, helping Leah to her feet as the smoking pendant began to vibrate, drawing the stunned Ameedis out of their slumber ... *not* the vision the classmates were expecting to see.

Locking their target once more, they swarmed towards the buckled shield of light, the danger retracting the moment Ethan whispered 'Ertigo', drawing a painful screech from the vampiric enemy. The incantation caused the crack in the smoking pendant to widen, signalling an end to the morning's entertainment as the Ameedis spun out of control.

Helpless to resist, the static enemy floated towards the penchant's hypnotic force field, sucked through the crack in the mirror. A burst of applause rang through the chamber, the crowd of onlookers deactivating their Velinis charms as the fountain of remedies stabilised, spinning elegantly in the centre of the space.

"Impressive," stated the young man who'd caused the havoc. "I thought you might come unstuck."

"It was Tom's quick thinking," Leah said, showing an interest in the thin, pale boy for the first time.

She knew he was a Koll, and that his uncle had been an infamous wizard, but he'd clearly inherited the *good* parts of his family's magical lineage. He was bright, intense and loyal, helping his friends out of trouble when he could have just protected himself.

"Well, Tom, it's fair to say you've impressed," Jalem added, introducing himself as he did. "Sorry about the vampire birds. It was part of the test."

"No harm done," Tom replied with a smile, happy he'd had a chance to prove himself and, more importantly, the *good* in him. He knew others had their suspicions, having a natural prejudice towards the family name, but he was determined to prove them wrong.

"You're our teacher's friend," Ethan stated, studying the tall, lithe figure in front of them.

"Yes," Jalem replied as the crowds came over to congratulate the classmates, "and glad to have helped today. It beats cataloguing charms."

"Sounds boring."

"It is," Jalem added with a smile, wondering if deciding against more adventurous pursuits had been the right one.

"You should come and visit sometime," Ethan suggested. "Maybe have a ride on a Williynx."

"I might just do that," Jalem stated as the Society elders voiced their approvals, shaking the hands of the classmates, leaving Jalem to make his exit, excited about the idea of taking to the skies on a Williynx: an experience that might tempt him towards more dangerous living.

"Maybe use your star again now," Roan suggested, experiencing the white insects' strangling sensation for the second time.

Relaxing in the grip of the Doveflies had worked last time - in the trading lane of Tallis & Crake — but not now, probably because of the influence their strange guide had over the white insects, Ilina orchestrating proceedings from below.

"It won't work," Ava suggested, pulling at the white strings around her neck, released by the army of insects.

'Why not?" Olin asked.

"Because it will make things worse. We're trapped and need to get out of this web *quickly*,"

"So, we vanish," Roan suggested, but this got another shake of the head from Ava.

"That's quitting and we're here to prove ourselves. You need to work out what your bovies do: your orb of light and Roan's gold pin."

"Well, we're being *strangled to death* so it's probably not the best time to work that out," Roan added with a touch of sarcasm.

"Then check out," Ava countered, "but you've already failed in Heaven's Chamber. Do you want another mark against your name?"

"So, give us a clue."

"Magneia," Roan whispered, staring at the gold pin as he did. He had no other ideas, deciding arguing wouldn't solve anything.

The pin stretched seconds later, remaining connected to his hand as it did, elongating as it formed a pole across the centre of the space they hovered in, the young lady bewitching them looking on from below. As the golden pole touched the walls on either side of them, Roan said, "Grab on and hope for the best," knowing this alone would unlikely save them.

"Wait," Olin countered, hoping his act of faith would work. "Let me grab on first with this." Nodding to the orb of light, he added, "I've got no idea if it will work, but we need to be free of the insects grip first."

With a nod from Ava and Roan, Olin placed his left hand on the pole, watching as the orb of light illuminated it, causing a glimmering curtain to fall below, the white insects drawn to the curtain of light, loosening their grip on the classmates' bodies.

The white strings fell away from the trio's arms, legs and necks, allowing them to breathe freely again as the decorative curtain offered an acceptable exit. Disappearing wasn't the answer, as Ava had explained, so another magic trick was necessary, using Roan and Olin's bovies to escape the clutches of a delicate enemy while an interested party looked on.

"We slide down, letting the insects connect to us again," Olin suggested, gesturing to the curtain of strings attaching to the wall of light.

"What?" Roan queried, not liking the idea of being strangled for a *third* time. "Let's just glide along the pole."

"No," Ava countered. "Olin's right. The insects were sent by a Society ally, meaning they're more likely to be guides than enemies. The fact they attached to Olin's orb of light reinforces this."

"It's some sort of clue to our future adventures," Olin added as Ilina looked on from below. "Also, no one else looks worried," Olin added, gesturing to comrades passing on flying bicycles, expressing little concern with their predicament.

"And she's *leaving*," Ava added, pointing to Ilina as she

moved towards the illustrated wall, "so we need to get a move on."

The idea that their guide's exit signalled the end of their lesson was enough, falling in unison as they grasped onto the curtain of white strings, feeling the insects attach to their bodies once more. As Olin had suggested, there was no suffocating grip this time, just a gentle weave of magic around their waists as they fell, spinning slowly as bicycles passed along the golden pole: a sign they had successfully aligned themselves to their prizes.

16

WISE GUIDES

"Impressive," Jacob commented as the group reconvened in The Illustrated Quarter.

"Thanks," Olin said, smiling at the discovery of another wonderland.

"I was talking about Harvey," Jacob joked, getting a sarcastic smile from his friend.

"Very funny," Harvey replied, a little subdued after his run-in with Katie and Tilly. "You didn't tell me they had secret weapons."

"He sort of did," Jalem countered, walking alongside Harvey as they wandered through another part of The Society Sphere. "You know, the *bovie* every student had."

"*Weapons* more like it," Harvey added, sweat still pouring down his face, "and some people *choose* to be Society soldiers."

"You played your part perfectly," Jacob stated as the group of students and accompanying guides nodded to passersby. "The aim was to give the students a taste of battle, and you did just that."

"It was fun," Ethan said, happy to know his smoking

pendant *absorbed* enemies. "Will we have more lessons like that?"

"Lessons in practical magic, you mean?"

Ethan nodded, adding, "Yes. I think we'll learn faster this way."

"Agreed," Ilina commented, pausing alongside Jacob beneath a bridge decorated in typical fashion. "There's nothing like learning on the job."

"So, you're learning as well?" Katie queried, wondering how Jacob's friends could be so at ease with magic.

"Yes, Katie; we're in the same boat as you — apprentices learning our trade."

"But you're older."

"And not necessarily wiser," Jalem offered with a smile, his elegant demeanour getting the attention of the girls. "Think of us as wise guides ... friends when you need a helping hand."

"You're the lady we met earlier," Tilly said, studying Ilina's restored features.

"Indeed I am, Katie. I'm glad the disguise worked."

"A disfigurement charm."

"Yes."

"Can I try it sometime?"

"Not until you've graduated," Jacob interjected, flicking his Vaspyl into the air to create a ladder towards the illustrated bridge. "Anyway, time for a bit more fun. Vaspyls at the ready."

With that, the group followed Jacob's lead, turning morphing steel into a ladder to the heavens ... each ladder snaking upwards until it disappeared into the illustration above them. As they rose on the twisting ladders of silver, Olin was already planning his next visit, keen to explore the wonderland of fun without the pressure of Society trials.

For now, he kept his balance as the ladders rose, lifting through the illustration of what looked like a fairground ride, witches and wizards spinning in loops as they whizzed past in every direction. The fun became more apparent once they were perched on the periphery of the attraction, like riders waiting to enter the fray.

It was simple and delightful all at once, the sight of Society members kneeling in position, waiting to sweep into a race as their ladders turned into tracks ... tracks that dipped and looped before cutting right and left ... the only thing holding them up the magnetic force of their ladders created from morphing steel.

Free of a need to prove themselves again, The Fateful Eight laughed in delight at the sight of Society elders letting their hair down, light laughter ringing in the air as they swooped up and down. How anyone could get bored with the S.P.M.A. was beyond Ava, clapping in delight as Harvey, Jalem and Ilina prepared for take off.

"Last one to The Singing Quarter buys the drinks all night," Ilina said, offering Jacob a smile as the trio took off, dipping suddenly as their silver ladders morphed into tracks ... tracks that catapulted them into a maze of delight as hundreds of witches and wizards passing one another ... some lifting off their silver pathways like seasoned veterans ... wise guides who'd return when the time was right.

"Can we come back soon?" Tom asked, eager to join the fun.

"You're free to come back anytime you like, assuming you don't finish last," Jacob replied with a mischievous smile.

"Where to?"

"The Seating Station," Jacob replied, adding, "the last

person to be seated gets homework as a reward: no vanishing charms allowed."

"*Sir,*" the class moaned in unison.

"You never set us homework," Ava commented as their ladders jolted into life, sending them hurtling into a ride of a lifetime.

"I must be in a good mood!" Jacob shouted as they plunged lower, circling one another before they darted off in different directions.

They used their feet to navigate their way, yells of delight emanating from them as they span in loops, realising charms weren't part of this adventure, the ride lifting them higher until they had a panoramic vision of The Illustrated Quarter: a new world of adventure awaiting the lucky few.

THE ONLY PERIUM ALLOWED WAS THE ONE FORMED AT THE END of the ride, perfect circles of steel transporting them home. The explosion of activity sent some Cendryll members scuttling for cover, relaxing at the sight of eight familiar faces scrambling towards The Seating Station.

Enjoying the injection of youth into their magical realm, the Society elders looked on with amusement as the students darted between the crowds, barging each other out of the way to avoid being last. Space was made by the more studious members, sensing the urgency in the game ... a game in danger of becoming violent as Ethan swung for Tom after being elbowed out of the way.

In the end, neither boy had to worry as one of them still hadn't returned — Katie reappearing moments later, sliding along the marble floor in pain, Jacob's face signalling a problem.

"UNDILUM!" the Society crowds uttered at once, arms lifted to remove the charm dragging Katie's body one way then the other ... the collective enchantment stopping Katie's erratic momentum.

It was the second close call now, Jacob knew, kneeling down to check on Katie's condition — the first one being Tilly's temporary trip to Quibbs Causeway after a Disira charm had backfired. The difference this time was *intent*. Katie had been 'under the influence' as Society members liked to call it, some form of troubling magic that she was unable to escape.

Gorrah (black magic) was rarely witnessed these days, but none were foolish enough to believe it had been eradicated. After all, it had been the shifting principle that saved the Society in the last war: the understanding that darkness had to negotiate to be understood.

The difference now, though, was that it had been used on a child without cause by a person without motive, or so it seemed.

"A little distance should help," came the familiar voice of an ageing giant: Kerevenn. "Step back, please," he added, his stooped figure dressed in sombre grey.

Originating from Sad Souls, Kerevenn was a Ulux — the name for the ageing giants of that realm. Blessed with a healing touch, the Ulux administered necessary remedy to those in need, typically Society members who'd fallen foul of The Orium Circle.

Whoever had cursed Katie was about to join that group, Jacob surmised, fighting a rising anger as he followed Kerevenn to the lift, calling Ethan towards him as he dismissed the others.

"There's a balance to restore," Jacob explained, the shadow of anger crossing his face enough to quell Ethan's protests. "We only use violence in exceptional circumstances, meaning the punch you threw at Tom needs to be sanctioned."

Ethan followed the adults to the lift, increasingly worried for Katie, laying statuesque in Kerevenn's arms. He hadn't seen anything in their ride home, no spark of sorcery decorating the air, so *how* had it happened and by who? Also, what did it mean for future explorations beyond The Cendryll.

"You'll stay with Katie until she recovers, finding out anything you can," Jacob added, taking off his Society tie as they entered the lift. "View this as your homework for the evening."

"Is she going to be okay?" Ethan asked, studying the rows of buttons in the lift.

"Yes, in time, but to save us all time we need information."

"Are we in danger then?"

"I doubt it, but someone has an axe to grind."

"So, it's not serious?"

"No, Ethan; it's more of a statement to get our attention."

"From who?"

"Precisely the question you need to answer?"

"Me?"

"Well, at the moment you're the only person exhibiting violent tendencies."

"You think *I* did it?"

"I think you need to find *who* did it. Darkness has no place in a wizard's heart, Ethan Lyell, especially wizards in the S.P.M.A. Reflect on your impulsive act and keep an eye on Katie. Kerevenn will do the rest."

With that, Jacob stepped out of the lift, leaving Ethan in the company of an ageing giant and lifeless classmate, wondering how much damage he'd done to his chances.

"Nothing a little remedy can't solve," Kerevenn explained with a warm smile, twisting the flower in the pocket of his grey shirt.

"Do you think it's serious? What happened to Katie, I mean."

"No, but the consequences could be."

"For the person who did it?"

"For those involved."

"Us, you mean. The Fateful Eight?"

With a nod, Kerevenn dabbed at his mouth with a tissue. "There are some that will always resist change, even to the point of putting their place in the S.P.M.A. at risk."

"So, they make a point through Katie."

"Yes."

"And now I've got to find out who the culprit is."

"With a little help from a friend," Kerevenn replied with a smile, pressing another button to send them jolting sideways, leading them on another ride into the dark recesses of The Cendryll, where gravity ended and a mystery began.

The room they entered was in another part of the building's fabric, Ethan realised, recognising no feature of the room. There was no circular balcony outside nor were there any Quij fluttering nearby, the luminous insects decorating each part of the faculty for charms.

Instead, they stood in an unspectacular room lined with colour running along the floor ... fine lines of colour representing the remedies needed for Katie's recuperation. Each line formed around one another to form a carpet effect, Kerevenn instructing Ethan to stand back from the lines of liquid.

Ethan wondered how long they were going to be cooped up in the room, concerned for Katie's recovery while also dwelling on his moment of madness. He knew why he'd swung for Tom, angry at what he perceived to be unfair treatment from Jacob.

Tom got away with *everything*, Ethan believed, using his sad state and family history to his advantage. His uncle was Erent Koll, the dark wizard who caused havoc a while ago. Mistakes were put down to Tom's sensitive nature, as if he was the only one weighed down by history.

Maybe they'd forgotten Ethan was related to *Weyen Lyell*, a member of The Orium Circle who had suffered serious injuries in the last war. If Casper Renn ruled The Cendryll, Weyen Lyell was the voice of the S.P.M.A. as a whole: two figures linked by Caribbean ancestry and magical blessings.

Ethan wasn't sure he had such blessings, but he needed to prove himself worthy sooner rather than later, realising swinging for his classmates wasn't the answer. If he continued like this, he'd end up isolated and alone, struggling to find his place in a group who were finding their feet as the days passed.

His chance to redeem himself started now, he knew, sitting by Katie's bedside as the liquid rivers flowed upwards ... towards her penchant necklace ... ready to trace a traitor's steps.

17

WITCHES' BREW

As the day passed in the company of Kerevenn, Ethan studied the multi-coloured remedies infusing Katie's penchant necklace. The ageing giant wouldn't explain the process, rather suggesting Ethan pay close attention to magic at work. *What* magic was at work was unclear to him, pulling his chair closer to the bed to get a closer look.

As far as he could tell, each remedy was regulating Katie's breathing, removing whatever spell had hypnotised her. Kerevenn was right, Ethan concluded. Katie was going to be okay and they weren't in danger; well, not yet at least. With the silence of the room weighing on him a little, Ethan decided to take out his pendant: the prize won on their midnight adventure through various Society buildings.

Maybe it could help him now, tasked with identifying the culprit putting Katie in this state. He knew the crack in the mirror absorbed creatures, smiling at the memory of the Ameedis screeching into oblivion, but wondered if it could do other things. For example, could it absorb *all* bad things...? Like a questionable spell enacted on a friend...?

"You have more gifts than you realise," Kerevenn said as he sat alongside his companion, "although you still doubt yourself."

"I'm not sure about that," Ethan replied, turning the pendant over in his right hand. "I've got a gift for messing up, that's for sure."

"You panic at critical moments, relying on instinct or guidance," Kerevenn explained, offering Ethan a vial of white liquid. "Semphul for hunger — nothing sinister."

"Thanks."

"Each of you is burdened in a way," Kerevenn continued, wiping his mouth with a tissue. "You have a great-uncle watching your every move, while others move in the shadows of more infamous relatives."

"Tom," Ethan uttered, flushing with embarrassment at the memory of swinging for him.

"Indeed. A boy who views the Koll name as a curse, forgetting that a certain relative remained loyal until the end."

"Who?"

"Prium Koll. A Melackin who triggered the hunt for a lethal artefact."

"The Terrecet."

"Yes, Ethan. It's a famous story now."

"Prium refused to give up the names or locations of certain youngsters, choosing a brutal death over betrayal. Tom chooses to dwell on a shadow rather than taking pride in a Melackin turned martyr: a man who become critical to the Society's survival."

"You're saying I'm doing the same," Ethan added. "Focusing too much on famous relatives."

"Yes, Ethan ... burdened by a greatness you're desperate to replicate. Of course, none of us are replicas so focus on what you *sense* and *know*. In the end, this is a magic of its own kind."

"I know I'm losing friends in my class, always wanting to be the best and finish first."

"Although when you put yourself first, you come last," Kerevenn replied with a smile, encouraging Ethan to drink the white remedy. He was strikingly tall but delicate in movements and mannerisms: a Ulux with a healing touch. "It's surprising what humility can bring to you, particularly in moments of crisis."

"I'm sort of in a crisis now, having to find out who did this to Katie."

"Then ask for help."

"From who?"

"Or what."

"*What?*" Ethan queried, his puzzled look drawing a smile from the ageing giant.

"You've discovered something of your pendant's powers, but sense there may be more."

"Is there?"

"Trust what you *sense* and *know*, Ethan Lyell," Kerevenn repeated, "remembering that magic exists *within* as much as *beyond*."

It was all the reassurance he needed, flicking open the pendant to study the cracked mirror inside. He'd thrown the object towards the vampiric army, threatening to rip them to pieces earlier, but knew this wasn't the strategy required now.

Katie was still unconscious, breathing more lightly as more colourful remedies ran into her penchant stone, the multi-coloured liquids arcing like a fountain of protective energy above her. Placing the pendant onto her might work, Ethan surmised, trusting it only absorbed enemy fire. What it would do was uncertain, but he knew it would do *something* ... something to help him on his quest for redemption ... in the eyes of Jacob, at least.

Placid and infinitely patient, Jacob hadn't taken kindly to Ethan's impulsive act, viewing his repressed violence as a potential problem. Jacob knew where unresolved anger could lead, wondering if this was the first mistake of many. It could be viewed as something and nothing, he realised, a reckless act typical of youthful volatility, but he also couldn't ignore the warning signs ... of a boy too keen to impress and too rash in his reactions.

Sofina had said as much after their midnight quest, searching for bovies in Society Square. Too many of the students had needed help, she commented, pushing Jacob to accept the obvious: that some of the students weren't destined for magical living. Jacob didn't disagree, but neither was he going to be pushed into making snap decisions.

After all, if a person's flaws marked them as incapable, there wouldn't be a single witch or wizard in the S.P.M.A. Sofina herself had a famous temper, resorting to a strangulation charm when she was particularly annoyed — the fate of the young girl in Founders' Quad who had already lost her place in the magical universe.

It was the girl who was on Ethan's mind as he placed the pendant on the bed, hoping he was right to trust his senses, just as Kerevenn had suggested he should. When he'd looked into the mirror, he'd seen a fleeting vision of youth ... a group of girls running towards Wimples with one girl turning to look back ... the girl gasping for breath outside Wimples a few days ago.

It was the day they'd met Sofina Blin on Horsel Hill: the witch with a penchant for strangulation. It was a public humiliation, Ethan reflected, the mother of the girl scrambling to get to her daughter: a member of the S.P.M.A. playing the role of oblivious above-ground parent, powerless to stop the pain. Ethan hadn't got a clear look at the woman but remembered the girl's face, knowing this was linked to Katie's condition.

Did the smoking pendant have multiple powers, identifying danger before obliterating it? It had sucked the life out of the Ameedis in The Illustrated Quarter, and now it was drawing him closer to a puzzle he needed to solve: the whereabouts of a magician with a grudge.

"Do you see now?" Kerevenn asked as the pendant released white smoke, opening to reveal the mirror inside just as Katie opened her eyes.

Staring at the mirror like a person possessed, Katie let out a deep breath, sitting up slowly. "Where am I?" she asked, struggling to clear her vision.

"In a safe place," Kerevenn replied with a smile, helping Katie to sit up.

"Have we done something wrong?" she asked Ethan.

"No, Katie," he replied. "You got caught by something on our way back from The Illustrated Quarter — or someone."

"A lady whispering something as I whizzed past," Katie added. "She followed me as we neared the end of the ride, smiling in a weird way. That's all I remember. But she's *there* in the mirror."

Pointing to the cracked mirror, Katie turned to Ethan who had found the clue he needed, sensing the lady and the choking girl were connected ... two images in a mirror with the ability to draw enemies to it. The girl wasn't an enemy, obviously, having no memory of her brief time in the S.P.M.A., but the mother was on the verge of becoming one, making the mistake of targeting a child to make a point.

"She looks pretty angry," Ethan stated, studying the frail lady in the mirror, traces of resentment lining her face.

"Well, she didn't have to take her anger out on me," Katie added, thankful to be back in the land of the living.

"You represent a symbol," Kerevenn explained, studying the river of remedies circling Katie's bare feet.

"Of what?"

"Youth and opportunity."

"Jocelyn is aggrieved that her daughter was robbed of this opportunity; the one you're living now."

"But she blabbed," Katie replied, wondering what spell had been used on her.

"Indeed she did, Katie, but children have done worse — Jacob's sister being a case in point."

"The Fire Witch," Ethan whispered, wondering what adventure Guppy Grayling was on now, a legend before reaching the official age of wizardry.

"A Fire Witch who set a precedent some years ago," Kerevenn explained, uttering 'Canvia' as he sketched an outline of buildings crashing through the ground. "Guppy made the mistake of following a stranger to Dyil's Ditch, strictly prohibited and almost getting herself and others killed."

"But she was let off," Katie added, following Kerevenn's train of thought. "That's why the lady's angry, because her daughter didn't get a second chance."

"But Guppy didn't try to *expose* the Society," Ethan countered. "How did she end up in Dyil's Ditch anyway?"

"Via a Cympgus," Kerevenn replied. "A portable Perium she hadn't quite grasped. Jocelyn, no doubt, is going to bring this up when she's brought in."

"Brought in?" Katie queried, her interest piqued at the idea of a drama unfolding. "By who?"

"By the two of you," the ageing giant replied with a smile, tapping his right foot three times.

"Why me?" Katie protested, concerned she hadn't returned to full health. "I've just been zapped by the woman. Maybe she won't be as gentle next time."

"I can go on my own," Ethan said, standing at the sound of the lift approaching. "I just need to borrow someone's Follygrin."

"Have mine," Katie replied, uttering 'Comeuppance' to retrieve the circular notebook: a pocket surveillance device.

Neither had mentioned their mild falling out, Ethan distancing himself from Katie after she revealed a ruthless side on top of Heaven's Chambers. He wasn't ignorant to the irony of judging his classmate, close to attacking Tom on their way back from The Illustrated Quarter. Perhaps they were both in jeopardy, the Society elders no doubt knowing of their recent behaviour.

Whether it was Heaven's Chamber, The Illustrated Quarter or a simple stroll above ground, whatever was said and done was watched ... society soldiers only ever a step away to counter false steps. One false step would land them in trouble, Ethan knew, either with their teacher or the woman they needed to find.

How they were supposed to bring her in was another puzzle, the sight of Kerevenn stepping into the lift suggesting he wasn't about to offer the answer.

"Dinner is served at eight in memory of our fallen comrades; an annual affair the Society takes very seriously. Smart dress and your best behaviour. Good luck," Kerevenn offered in a parting gesture, the wise guide they would be without on their new hunt.

"Dinner?" Katie queried, having no recollection of the commemorative event being mentioned — a reminder of how little they still knew about the rhythms and traditions of the S.P.M.A.

"Who knows," Ethan replied with a shrug.

"Have you done something?" Katie asked as she put on her shoes.

"What do you mean?" Ethan replied, sensing the tension between them.

"You just seem to be going along with this."

"I lost my temper earlier; I sort of went for Tom."

"*Went* for him?"

"I tried to punch him. He was getting on my nerves, barging me to make sure he didn't finish last."

"You hate finishing last."

"You can talk," Ethan countered, careful to modify his tone. "Anyway, this is probably our karma: payback for our obsession with winning."

"I've re-evaluated that," Katie added, letting her gaze fall onto the boy she secretly admired. "I was only anything if I won — at least to my parents — but it turned me into a person I didn't want to be. We might graduate and we might not, but we're going to have the time of our lives either way."

"Not that we'll remember it if we fail."

"But I think we'll remember the lessons," Katie stated. "Important lessons about friendship and honour. I get why you've backed away from me; I said stupid things in Heaven's Chamber."

"You sounded like you were willing to win at any cost."

"I was, but not now. What's the point of graduating without friends? Experiencing a spectacular world alone?"

"I could do with a friend now. Jacob's angry with me for trying to hit Tom, making it clear I need to solve the puzzle of who attacked you."

"Well, we've done that," Katie replied, tying back her blonde hair, "and now all we need to do is bring her in."

"Just like that," Ethan added with a smile, glad to return to familiar rhythms.

"Just like that," Katie said, linking arms with the friend she thought she'd lost. "Dinner's at eight and I need to miracle a dress from somewhere, so let's reacquaint ourselves with a brooding witch."

18
CLOSE CALL

The church roof was the chosen lookout, Ethan and Katie deciding this offered thinking time. Katie's Follygrin located Jocelyn Zucklewick in Society Square, roaming the streets alone. There was no sign of her daughter, Ellie, which seemed odd to Katie as if Jocelyn Zucklewick expected company.

The fact mother and daughter had been together above ground on two occasions — Ellie suffering a strangulation spell and the fun ride back from The Illustrated Quarter — suggested an absent father. This was an assumption, Katie knew, but a logical hypothesis under the circumstances.

No father figure had made an appearance so far, suggesting one of two things: they were busy at work in a Society faculty or they weren't around at all. Either way, the sight of Jocelyn wandering alone was at odds with her recent behaviour, striking out against a child knowing it would have consequences. The spell used was an Ankrya charm, having a hypnotic effect on its target.

It was more effective on inexperienced magicians, due to their limited knowledge of counter charms — the reason

Jocelyn had decided to use it on Katie as she whizzed along her steel tracks, arcing left and right before looping upwards into the bright sky.

On reflection, it was more of a statement than an attack, a collective Cendryll force releasing her from the spell in seconds. Now, it was time for two classmates to make a statement of their own, ready to make their presence known as the shops wound down to closing time.

As always, there were familiar faces above ground, blending into the crowds of shoppers, many of whom were none the wiser to a magical universe hiding in plain sight. That would always have to be the case, Ethan and Katie knew, wrapped up against the cold wind as they discussed their plan.

"Do you think she knows we're watching?" Ethan asked, loosening the scarf around his neck.

"Well, we've been spying on her so probably," Katie replied, deciding a coat was necessary on this occasion.

Aside from their journey to an ice chamber a few days ago, Katie never wore coats, choosing the simplicity of jeans and a T-shirt — partly a statement to prove her toughness. She'd learnt about the fragility of inflated egos since then, largely due to Tilly's wise words in The Cathedral of Stars.

Humility would get her further than arrogance, she knew now, wondering if this was the reason she and Ethan had ended up together now: the duo convinced of their magical talents until recently.

"So, what's the plan?" Katie prompted, keen to get off the church roof.

"Appear in the next shop she goes into, then find a way to drag her through a Perium."

"*Drag her?*"

"*Encourage* her, using some of the charms we've learnt."

"Any particular charm in mind?"

"The one she used on you," Ethan suggested.

"I'm sure she knows the counter spell."

"Not if we use the Vyoxal charm to shut her up," Ethan replied with a smile. "If she can't speak, she can't activate spells."

"Quick thinking, Ethan Lyell," Katie added, offering a friendly nudge.

Whether they would ever be more than friends was uncertain, Katie aware that reforging their friendship was more important at the moment. Also, romantic thoughts could lead to distractions, the last thing they needed now. Ethan needed to prove a point to Jacob, and Katie needed to prove something to herself ... each on a personal mission of atonement as Jocelyn Zucklewick entered Lampsyl's Lotions.

"Time to say hello," Ethan quipped, turning towards the small door leading them off the church roof. Out of sight of above-ground eyes, 'Whereabouts' was uttered, creating a portable Perium — ropes of yellow light glittering in front of them, offering the final ride of the day.

"What if we crash land in the middle of the shop?" Ethan asked as they grabbed onto the ropes of light.

"We'll be packing our bags," Katie replied, confident this wouldn't be the outcome.

A Cympgus was a simple form of magical transportation, requiring the user to imagine their desired location. Lampsyl's Lotions was designed like most Society buildings, its interior space far greater than the external facade suggested. Magic had few limits, after all, meaning they simply had to imagine the room stretching beyond the shop frontage, lined with lotions to heal all ailments: touched by magic, of course.

The room of lotions was rarely occupied, hidden from above-ground eyes and only accessed by the family who ran it. Conditioned in the ways of magical travel, the family were used to magicians appearing in the secret part of the shop.

It would come down to timing, Ethan knew, conscious of the need to engage Jocelyn Zucklewick inside the shop. *How* this could be done in view of non-magical folk was the final puzzle, something he continued to ruminate over as they swung on their ropes of light, giggling at the wonder of it all.

The space they landed in was lined with colour, jars of lotions decorating the shelves that stretched as far as a football field. Lampsyl's Lotions was the place to remedy ailments, for above-ground folk at least, offering immediate relief from pain. It was also a good strike point, Ethan and Katie knew, able to appear in the shop front in seconds.

"So, I say we use the Vyoxal charm first," Katie suggested, rubbing her fingers in preparation. "Remove her ability to protest, meaning we draw no attention to ourselves."

"Good plan," Ethan replied as they walked through the cluttered space, "then we need to find a way to manoeuvre her out of view."

"Which will be the difficult part."

"A Fixilia charm?"

"Freezing her to the spot will *definitely* draw attention to us," Katie countered, adding, "a Soppori charm will be less obvious."

"A sleep charm to make it look like she's fainted," Ethan added with a smile. "You're good, Katie Follygrin."

"I have my moments. Come on, let's get a move on before she vanishes."

With that, the friends stepped towards the large, oak

door, placing their hands on the brass handle and turning it anti-clockwise ... the sound of locks turning followed by a mild vibration ... leading them into the busy shop front of Lampsyl's Lotions ... where the frail and feverish clamoured for attention.

"She's near the door," Katie whispered, gesturing to the figure of Jocelyn Zucklewick studying the busy streets. "It's a game; she's trying to force a mistake from us so we end up facing the same fate as her daughter."

"If she leaves, we've got a bigger problem," Ethan added, concerned they were going to fail this test, leading to more stern looks from Jacob.

"Don't make eye contact," Katie suggested as one of the hyperactive shop owners eased past them, using a ladder to get the required lotion. "Wait for her to make her move."

The move came subtly ... the sound of vibrations filling the shop ... vibrations that built as jars began to wobble on the shelves ... causing looks of unease. Crowds gathered outside as the first jars fell to the floor, exploding warm liquid everywhere as people rushed for the exit, leaving Jocelyn Zucklewick to study the carnage.

"Now what?" Ethan asked, realising that they needed to act before it was too late.

"Wait until the shop clears, then we can reacquaint ourselves."

Their plan was helped by the shop owners, busily ushering the last customers out before locking the door, allowing a trio of magicians to iron out their differences. Obviously aware of recent events, the family who ran the shop uttered 'Mirriul', standing together behind the counter as various images appeared on the windows — images of them clearing up the mess as the two children and static lady began a conversation.

This wasn't quite how events played out, Ethan and Katie activating an invisibility charm to ensure their movements were hidden from prying eyes. It helped that Society folk were ushering onlookers away, dressed in uniforms suggesting some semblance of authority. There were many rumours about such figures, including a well-worn one about a secret sect with ties to the government.

This wasn't so far from the truth except for the binding principle of magic, something no ordinary resident had ever considered. It was Ethan and Katie's job to ensure things stayed this way, uttering different charms the moment Jocelyn flicked a spark of light towards them.

With the Mirriul charm doing its job of providing adequate cover, Ethan used the Fixilia charm to prevent their target from leaving, whilst Katie removed her ability to speak via the Vyoxal charm, leading to a violent reaction as the jars exploded, sending a shower of glass onto the classmates: time to repay a small favour.

Such a public display was dangerous, turning rumour into fear, something the Society could not afford to happen, leading to a collective countermeasure. The family running the shop opened the door to the cavern of lotions, tilting the floor as they did so ... a move that enabled Ethan and Katie to tighten their grip on a new enemy ... Jocelyn releasing a silent shout as she exploded more jars ... until a collective whisper of 'Ankrya' rendered her powerless.

Under normal circumstances, she would have enacted the counter charm, dismissing the hypnotic powers of the Ankrya charm, but she had a force to reckon with now, including an increasingly angry family of shop owners who had a mess to clean up.

"Get her behind the door," the father of the family

instructed, his black suit and curled moustache reminded Ethan of a Victorian gentleman. "We'll do the rest."

The door in question was the one they'd entered through, the large oak door providing the privacy they needed. Before long, someone would be knocking on the shop window, more interested in easing their pain than the drama within.

Things happened in Society Square, the above-ground world knew, but things happened in every part of the world, and as long as their beloved quarter continued to offer delights, they were happy to live in ignorant bliss.

With the first phase of engagement successfully executed, Ethan and Katie struggled with the power of Jocelyn Zucklewick's will. Despite being restricted from counter fire and under the influence of a hypnotic charm, she continued to fight against her constraints, humming incantations that couldn't be spoken ... spells that had no effect on Katie this time.

Like Sofina Blin's strangulation spell on the woman's daughter, the Ankrya charm did no lasting damage providing it was used to constrain. This was the principle of all Society sorcery, only to be used when necessary and never with inappropriate force. Peace continued to be the fundamental principle of magical living, despite the fact problems continued to present themselves.

Jocelyn Zucklewick was the current problem, her exploding trick likely to have severe consequences. A mild attack on a child was one thing, but threatening to expose a centuries-old magical Society was something else entirely ... consequence closing in as she continued to struggle against her captors.

"Stay against the walls," the moustached proprietor instructed, gesturing for his family to take their positions.

His wife and two children standing at one end of the room, arms pointed towards the culprit as the floorboards snapped ... creating a crevice for Jocelyn Zucklewick to sink into ... the sight of a flurry of Quij signalling her destination.

"Do we jump through?" Katie asked, anchoring herself to a wall with the Magneia charm.

"Probably," Ethan replied, walking up the wall towards the ceiling, remembering Kerevenn's advice to trust what he *knew* and *sensed*. He knew he had to win back Jacob's trust, sensing the Quij's appearance signalled something. The family were in control of things now, but it was Ethan and Katie's job to bring the culprit in, leading him to decide on a rash move, hanging upside down on the ceiling. "I say we jump."

"Why?" Katie queried, not sensing the same need for a dramatic return.

"Because it looks like we're bystanders."

"We're being watched, Ethan."

"And I'm being judged. Trust me, Katie; we need to jump."

"Okay, but don't start punching people if this goes wrong."

"Very funny," Ethan replied as jars rattled on the shelves, threatening to topple into the hole in the floor ... floorboards cracking and splintering as Jocelyn lost her battle with a superior force.

"*Now,*" Ethan said, releasing the Magneia charm as he descended with Katie, signalling thanks to the Society family who'd helped him prove his worth.

As they fell through the gap, the Quij followed, the luminous insects resting on Jocelyn's eyes, drawing a silent scream from a mother on the verge of a painful rehabilitation.

19
JUDGEMENT DAY

Strings of light decorated The Cendryll, courtesy of the Quij, the beautiful insects forming a commemorative light for the annual Society dinner. The ground floor was less crowded than normal, witches and wizards preparing for the evening event. A few familiar faces sat at The Seating Station, though, including a group the students had only heard of until now: The Orium Circle.

The Orium Circle were the most senior members of the S.P.M.A., forming and imposing all laws in the Society — bad news for Jocelyn Zucklewick who'd given up her struggle at the sight of the six figures many feared. With Jacob, Casper and Philomeena also present, it was clear judgement was about to be handed down.

As the Quij continued to form strings of light, creating a chandelier effect around the skylight, the Society adults mused on the fate of the mother in their midst. Having an immaculate record until now, Jocelyn Zucklewick lay lifeless on the floor, still under the restrictive charms Ethan and Katie had activated: the two students hoping they'd atoned for poor choices made.

It was Weyen Lyell Ethan was preoccupied with, the flamboyant Caribbean figure standing alongside Jacob and Philomeena, discussing what should be done. Casper occupied the other members of The Orium Circle: a collection of men and women rarely seen beyond the magical faculty they called home.

Dominated by floating floors and surveillance devices known as Tabulals, The Orium was a spectacular triangular structure, offering welcome to a chosen few: Casper and Philomeena among them. It was now a delicate balancing act between consequence and compassion, Casper knew, always siding with compassion wherever possible.

Jocelyn's act was a statement in principle, Casper reinforced as the S.P.M.A. logo glowed on the marble floor, adding another decorative touch to the evening's proceedings. She had a right to be angry, considering the Society's willingness to forgive other underage wizards, Casper continued, directing his attention to Melina Guest who scribbled away in a notebook.

Philomeena was also arguing for compassion, whispering her points to Weyen Lyell who nodded, rubbing the enormous ring on his right hand: a ring decorated with a multi-coloured gemstone. Dressed in a purple suit, the man many feared held Philomeena's gaze, signalling an intimacy between them.

It was a quiet romance punctuated by Society duty, but an intense love nonetheless, the Society legends capturing moments in romantic realms: The Cathedral of Stars being one of their favourites. Romance wasn't on the agenda this evening, however, the fate of Jocelyn Zucklewick needing to be resolved.

The commemorative dinner was less than an hour away, reinforced by the quiet that hovered over The Cendryll.

Usually a hive of activity with doors swinging to-and-fro, the faculty for charms became a temporary cell for a woman lost in resentment.

"Stand," Weyen Lyell instructed, stepping closer to Jocelyn.

With Ethan and Katie remaining in position, the other members of The Orium Circle looked on, moving away from The Seating Station to stand as one. Jocelyn Zucklewick stood slowly, conscious of the circle of fire formed around her feet ... an Infernisi charm formed by Casper and Philomeena to limit her movements.

Still restricted and powerless, escape was no longer an option for a woman who could be hunted down in seconds, her daughter at home with a father who'd received news of her mad act via a Scribberal: the silver communication rattling to signal bad news for the family.

"You've made an unfortunate choice, Jocelyn," Weyen began, circling to signal his intent, "and we all know where unfortunate choices lead."

The mother's silence was marked, suggesting a contempt for the Society lawmakers — a gesture she would soon regret. With a flick of the wrist, white mist formed around Jocelyn's silent figure, forcing her to gasp for air. Still unable to speak or move freely, she writhed in pain as Weyen continued to circle, unbuttoning his green coat as he did so.

The coat signifying Society royalty lifted at the hem, suggesting an impending fury but no violent act followed, merely the continuation of an interrogation: a sight driving home the consequences of fatal mistakes to Ethan and Katie.

They wondered where their classmates were, both wanting to discuss their recent adventure, but that thought vanished at the sight of the next move ... the white mist clinging to Jocelyn's body. Visibly in pain, she dropped to her knees, coughing as the first tears fell, the signal for the mild torture to stop.

"Humility may save you yet," Melina Guest commented as she continued to scribble in a notebook, her fire-red hair reaching below her waist.

She shared Weyen's flamboyant nature whilst often remaining in the background: the member of The Orium Circle some feared the most. Melina was Weyen's equal in many ways, listening to the views of the group before discussing its nuances with the imposing Caribbean figure.

It seemed the decision had already been made, Ethan thought, sensing where Jocelyn was going to end up whilst wondering what he could do to stop it. He also sensed that her scribbling represented Jocelyn's fate, recognising the notebook to be a Panorilum — the floating piece of parchment morphing into a surveillance device in seconds.

There were two options, Ethan knew — The Velynx or Sad Souls — neither leading to a compassionate outcome. The Velynx was the slime-covered prison for comrades turned villains, and Sad Souls was synonymous with rehabilitation. Rehabilitation was a kind way of putting it, Ethan knew, knowing the story of Jacob's mother: an ex-member of The Cendryll who now lived on the Society margins.

Melackin was the word on Ethan's mind, a lesser punishment than the Velynx but a life without magic, nonetheless. In some ways, rehabilitation was worse because Melackin remained in the magical world, scraping a living in the knowledge of what they'd thrown away.

With their powers removed, they could only dream of a return, knowing they were watched at all times, compassion only extending so far. Rehabilitation was kinder but still not what Ethan or Katie wanted, the friends sharing a glance to suggest something needed to be said.

"She didn't mean to hurt me," Katie stated, worried Jocelyn was going to choke to death. "She was just trying to make a point."

"And we're making ours," Weyen responded, turning his intense gaze onto Katie.

The large afro and glittering ring were symbols of glamour and power, both resting easily on royal shoulders.

"Maybe if we let her talk," Ethan suggested, gathering the courage to challenge his great uncle: the man whose shadow he'd lived in for so long.

"A brief explanation won't hurt," Philomeena added, placing a hand on Weyen's arm to remind him of the compassion he'd shown to others, namely Jacob and his younger sister some years ago.

Her niece, Kaira, also benefited from this reprieve, allowing her to grow into the young woman she was now: a warrior venturing through the many realms of the Society. It was a compassion Weyen remembered well, risking his reputation on three underage wizards who turned out to be vital to the Society's survival.

Perhaps it was a case of fate intervening again, he mused, studying his great-nephew and the girl who shared his competitive edge. They were on a similar trajectory to the one Jacob had been on, caught in a blizzard of wonder as events unfolded at a pace.

Whether they would prove themselves worthy was another matter, but for now they were hinting at the foresight another trio of wizards had displayed, formed in childhood innocence that held a magic of its own.

"Very well," Weyen relented, releasing the white mist

with a whispered incantation, adding "release her" to Ethan and Katie as he did.

Maintaining their positions, the classmates uttered 'Undilum' to deactivate the restrictive charms, joining Jacob who stood by The Seating Station, keeping a respectful distance from proceedings. Something about the ritual clearly bothered him, his unease evident in the way he studied the lines of light ... his connection to Society creatures well known amongst the class.

Jacob could call Quij and halt a Williynx's fury, Ethan knew, wondering at his teacher's distant manner. Perhaps his teacher didn't like unnecessary cruelty, marked by his early days in the S.P.M.A. Regularly bullied by a group known as The Sinister Four, Jacob remained sensitive to similar situations.

This wasn't quite bullying but it was intimidation, Jacob knew, keeping his distance to signal his distaste for certain methods. Little did Ethan and Katie know that their brief intervention had won favour with their teacher, offering a touch of compassion at a critical moment. It had altered his perception of the pair, making Jacob wonder if they could make the grade, after all.

"You're free to talk," Melina Guest stated, stepping closer to Jocelyn, the notebook in her hand thrown into the air, unfolding into a floating piece of parchment: the surveillance device to illustrate future travel.

"Nothing I say will matter now," Jocelyn replied, her brown hair falling over her face as the tears continued to fall.

"It just might," Casper added, maintaining the ring of fire with his sister, Philomeena. "Peace is always the aim of our world as you know Jocelyn, so take the opportunity offered, remembering it came from the child you attacked."

"A simple spell to get your attention," Jocelyn explained, holding Casper's gaze as the ring of fire rose around her, "and here we are."

"Indeed," Weyen stated, rubbing the large ring on his right hand. "With your future on the line, so state your case because time is against you."

"You know my position," Jocelyn continued. "You all do! You have different rules for different people. Take Casper's daughter, Kaira. How many mistakes did *she* make along with *him* and his *amazing* sister? Were *they* banished with their memories wiped? *Of course not.*

They were *rewarded* with increased training and access to secrets *no other members had.* Taken into the heart of the Society as war rose on the horizon. Now, you all stand here in your positions of power, *torturing* and *humiliating* me because I made a stand!? You talk of peace but flaunt your power when it suits, selecting the young based on bias and family influence.

I wonder, will *Ethan Lyell* make the grade, Weyen? Your great-nephew who *surely* couldn't embarrass the family name. So do as you please. Choke me with your magic and show me my fate on that piece of parchment. *Punish* my family *even more* while you decorate The Cendryll for a commemorative dinner.

My husband and daughter will suffer without me and it will be *your doing. Your cross to bear* if anything happens to them. Peace is the pretence you perpetuate, wielding your power where and when you want, so carry on with your performance and I'll be the willing audience."

"A powerful speech and not without a semblance of truth," Larell Follygrin stated, the most distant member of The Orium Circle, and the one most likely to choose sanctions over salvation. What he said next surprised the gathering. "Perhaps we should let the children decide, since they haven't shown the bias you suggest. Children who have argued for leniency. What would they choose?"

As all eyes turned towards Ethan and Katie, Jacob was reminded of the compassion shown to a lost boy recently: a boy who shook the foundations of a magical realm hidden in the stars.

"She could help to teach us," Katie suggested, shrugging at Ethan's look of surprise. "If she really wanted to hurt me, she would have so maybe it was all about *this* — a chance to get her point across to the most important people in the Society. I think Jocelyn's been honest and like you said, she's got a point."

"And Ethan?" Larell Follygrin prompted.

"Why not?" Ethan replied with another shrug. "I mean, if Sofina hadn't almost strangled her daughter, we probably wouldn't be here."

"A point well made," Philomeena echoed, catching Weyen's eye as he pondered a possible solution.

"On the condition that Jocelyn stays in The Cendryll until further notice," Weyen stated, his gaze resting on the classmates who'd suggested compassion as an alternative to punishment: the very thing they were seeking themselves.

"And maybe giving Jocelyn's daughter a second chance?" Katie added, feeling she may as well push her luck.

"That is unheard of," Melina Guest countered, unbuttoning her green coat as if she were about to strike out.

"So is forgiving an attack on a child," Casper challenged. "Ultimately, Jocelyn is right. We've forgiven worse, offering second chances to those we deemed worthy. It's a simple matter of starting again for Jocelyn's daughter. In the end, she did little more than whisper rumours to old friends —

friends whose memories have been altered. Should either trip up, then no blame can be laid at our door."

"Why?" Jocelyn Zucklewick asked, turning to Katie with a look of contrition: the girl she'd targeted to make a point.

"Because it's not always about winning," Katie replied, remembering the lesson Tilly had taught her in The Cathedral of Stars.

20

FRIENDSHIPS FORGED

With a mother's fate decided, Katie and Ethan joined their classmates on the third floor. Instructed to go to Ava's quarters, they were welcomed by Henry Blin.

"The warriors return," Ava's dad joked as he ushered them in, glancing at the chandelier-effect created by the Quij.

"So, what happened?" Tom asked, still a little uneasy around Ethan.

"They've been given a second chance," Katie replied, delighted by the sight of cakes on the table.

"*They*?" Leah queried, adding a flower to her hair.

The others were already dressed for the commemorative meal, Leah carrying off a sequinned-blue dress with ease as Tom adjusted the belt on his silver-grey suit.

"Jocelyn and her daughter, Ellie," Katie added.

"*What*?" Roan commented, more interested in the cakes than the tie Tilly was helping him with. "How does that work?"

"It was Ethan's idea," Katie said, offering her friend a smile.

"It was *our* idea," Ethan added, conscious of sharing the limelight. "Jocelyn said she only stunned Katie to make a point, gambling on The Orium Circle appearing to decide her fate."

"What point?" Tilly asked, her red hair complimenting her dark-green dress.

"That the Society had forgiven worse, naming Jacob's sister to suggest they favoured some families over others. The Orium Circle didn't know what to say about that, which is when the scary guy turned to us, asking us to make the decision."

"A member of The Orium Circle?"

Ethan nodded, explaining, "He didn't give his name but he looked *dangerous*."

"And you let them off?" Olin asked, making sure he'd heard his classmates right.

The most eccentric of the group, Olin stood in a three-piece tweed suit with a gold pocket watch to complete the look. He remained the most natural magician in the class, but hadn't forgotten about the spider appearing on his tongue a few days ago. He was in the very place they occupied now, listening to Henry Blin's description of the spider: a Vanarix.

The name was enough to signal something bad, and Olin had been thinking about it ever since. Would *he* turn out to be bad or was it an omen of something else? He was also surprised none of his classmates had mentioned it, hoping Roan and Ava hadn't brought it up. It had appeared for a reason, though, Ava's dad explaining that no Society creature was ever used in the magical sweets from Wimples.

Today was about commemorating the dead, however,

and getting to grips with the idea of forgiveness. If Ellie Zucklewick had been given a second chance — the first student to be banished for a loose tongue — it set a precedent for second chances, something Olin felt each member of the class would need.

"Everyone deserves a second chance," Ethan said, turning to Tom as he said this.

"Agreed," Tom echoed, looking handsome in his tuxedo. "I'm good at ducking punches, anyway."

Placing an arm around Ethan, Tom said, "Come on, I'll show you your outfit for the evening."

"You'll love it," Ava added with a mischievous smile, making Ethan think he probably wouldn't.

"And I'll show you yours," Tilly said to Katie, gesturing for her friend to follow her.

"So, it seems like we're all set," Henry Blin stated, enjoying the propellor effect of his bow tie: a touch of magic he couldn't resist.

He'd organised the children's outfits with the help of Philomeena Renn, a woman known for her elegance. If it had been left to Henry, he would have followed strict tradition but Philomeena suggested something else ... an outfit to reflect each student's character ... a decision which had gone down well with the class.

"When you say we have to be on our best behaviour," Ava prompted, glancing at her dad to elaborate.

"It's a formal dinner, Ava, with all the nuances of tradition."

"Meaning?"

"Meaning members from all faculties will be in attendance, some of whom have lost loved ones. The dinner is a celebration of legends as opposed to mourning the dead."

"What's the difference?" Olin asked, checking the time with his gold pocket watch.

"The Cendryll comes to life," Ava's dad replied with a smile, deciding to elaborate no further.

WITH EACH CLASSMATE DRESSED FOR THE OCCASION, HENRY led them out onto the third-floor balcony, nodding to crowds who passed by in a glittering array of costumes. A chandelier of light hung from the skylight, the Quij adding their own touch of glamour.

The main spectacle was the S.P.M.A. logo decorating the ground floor, glowing as it rotated as the doors turned into mirrors, the reflection of dead legends appearing in each. Roan recognised one of the faces, associating the wizard in question with a cousin's recent adventures. It was a reminder of the fragility of peaceful living, and the need to always be on guard.

The dead decorating the mirrors waved and smiled, suggesting they were at peace in whatever realm they rested in: a sight that caused unease in some. Most members of Jacob's class had lost a family member in recent times, the sudden reminder of this the final lesson of the day.

It was a sight most troubling to Katie, studying the frail, elderly figure propped up by a walking stick. The relative had sacrificed his life to protect a centuries-old secret, his granddaughter 'elsewhere' in an attempt to manage her grief.

It was a reminder to Katie of how things could end, hoping she would die honourably if the moment ever came. The first few months had taught her so much, distancing herself from her parents' preoccupation with status, helped by the wisdom of the red-headed girl she walked alongside now: Tilly Flint.

Tilly hadn't changed her mind on future plans, deciding to go along with things as long as they felt right. She shared the burden of parental expectation with Katie, but not the need to feed their desires. For Tilly, the magic would fade if she discovered it wasn't for her, ready to return to aboveground living if this was the case. Ultimately, none of them would remember their adventure if they failed, Tilly knew, wondering who else would be granted a second chance if they messed up.

Benches of light formed to interrupt Tilly's thoughts, floating in rows between the chandelier of light ... sky urchins appearing through the mirrors with a feast ... the scarred-ravaged creatures from The Wenlands placing plates, glasses and cutlery on the floating benches.

"Wicked," Ethan commented, dressed in a pink suit he'd initially refused to wear.

"If you want to offend Philomeena, wear your jeans," Tom had said, using all of his persuasive powers to talk Ethan into the idea.

"If you make fun of me, I *will* punch you," Ethan replied half playfully, surprised at the fit of the suit, complimented by a white shirt.

He wore it proudly now, getting a look of appreciation from Katie, secretly hoping for a dance although the layout of The Cendryll suggested no such thing.

"Where do we sit?" Ethan whispered, reaching out to touch the chandelier of light.

"Where you're instructed to," Henry replied, more taken by his spinning bow tie than the glamorous set up.

"By who?" Ava prompted.

"The sky urchins, of course."

It took a little time to read the rhythm of things, Olin studying the sky urchin hovering at the end of each bench, gesturing for certain crowds to sit. Flight charms were used to take the correct seating position, witches and wizards in flamboyant costumes floating through the air in silence, the principle of respecting the dead remaining at the heart of things.

"Try not to knock the glasses over," Roan whispered to Ava, deciding a little teasing of his friend would help to alleviate his nerves.

"I'm not the one shaking," Ava countered, looking resplendent in white.

"Off we go," Henry instructed, nodding for his daughter to go first, the utterance of 'Propellus Celiri' wrapping a flower around Ava's hand ... a propellor motion forming to lift her into the air ... directing her sail towards the bench closest to the skylight.

The others followed, thankful not to bump into anyone as they took their seats, the stars filling the skylight adding a final touch of beauty. With Henry and Jacob joining them, the class settled, studying the spectacle.

"You made it," Jacob said, sticking to tradition with a tuxedo.

"You mean we've all graduated," Roan quipped, eager to taste the array of food.

"You've survived the first phase," Jacob replied with a smile, "and discovered friendship and compassion along the way."

Ethan glanced at Jacob, hoping for a look of approval from the teacher he admired, something which came when the gathering stood, raising their glasses of colourful remedies.

"To the living and the dead," Casper said from the opposite bench, framed by the chandelier of light, "and to our youngest members: may magic always be there to guide you."

The final sentiment was repeated by the gathering, Jacob studying his students with pride — a mark of the progress they'd made in a Society of dreams. They had all impressed him at points, discovering things about themselves necessary to their progress, including Ethan and Katie who had recovered from a worrying start.

They had caused the most concern in the early days, too keen to impress and too often lacking contrition, but they'd made amends with Jocelyn, impressing The Orium Circle along the way. The class had more challenges ahead and greater dangers to negotiate, but for now they were part of the S.P.M.A., finding friendship in unlikely places and compassion at critical moments.

"They'll be okay," Henry commented as the students tucked into the feast, talking to sky urchins and ageing giants alike, the Quij continuing to shower the gathering with light.

"They're okay for now," Jacob replied, happy the class was enjoying the moment.

They *wouldn't* all be okay, of course, but that was for the future, Jacob thinking of Ilina: the girl who'd captured his heart and made him imagine life beyond The Cendryll: the home he would have to venture beyond to balance love with duty.

Duty was the focus for now, though, his class of eight students behaving as children should, without a care in the world. It was a youthful innocence Jacob remembered, smiling at the memory of his early days in The Cendryll. Then it was his sister, Guppy, who got them tangled up in mysteries beyond their years, leading to a raging mayhem they'd barely survived.

Survival was the name of the game in this episode of magical living, Jacob knew, parking thoughts of the difficult times ahead when laughter would fade and old resentments rise in his young class: the ultimate test of character to distinguish between the destined and the damned.

TEASER CHAPTER BOOK 2

The Fateful Eight waited in the fifth-floor classroom, ruminating on the new setup. In a few minutes, their teachers would arrive: Jacob Grayling and Jocelyn Zucklewick. Still bemused by Ethan and Katie's last-minute reprieve of Jocelyn, Tom pressed his classmates on what had led to their sudden burst of compassion.

"Like we said, everyone deserves a second chance," Ethan explained, smiling at Katie as he did.

The others noticed the smile, sharing looks that suggested a blossoming romance.

"Well, let's hope *we* get a second chance," Olin added, not as confident as he once was, realising everyone was operating at a similar level.

The smallest of the group and still the most astute, Olin had learnt that reserve wasn't always the answer, careful not to marginalise himself amongst his peers. After all, he was the one who'd had a spider appear on his tongue, something no one else had mentioned since.

He was hoping Ava and Roan had kept *that* event quiet, but kids had a habit of sharing gossip, making him wonder when the whispers of him being 'marked' would begin.

"If Jocelyn's daughter did, we should," Tilly echoed in reference to second chances.

"Unless this was all a ruse to mess things up for us," Roan suggested, sitting on the window ledge alongside Ava.

"You think she's out to get us?" Ethan questioned, uttering 'Spintz' to decorate the austere classroom. "A witch about to turn bad, turning on us at the first opportunity."

Ethan uttered 'Disira', vanishing out of sight before appearing on the windowsill alongside Roan, pretending to strangle him. "Operating like a ghost at night ..." he added in his most dramatic voice.

"I think the two of you should get together," Leah joked, offering the friends a smile. "I mean, Ethan's got the looks and you've sort of got the charm."

A comment that brought a bout of laughter from the class. Bonds had formed in their first few months, surviving their early trials whilst avoiding any major mishaps. Temporary wounds had also been healed, particularly between a certain trio: Ethan, Katie and Tom.

By far the most competitive, Ethan and Katie had learned humility the hard way, offering a dose to the woman about to appear through the big, wooden door with Jacob. Their early mistakes had been overlooked by Jacob and the Society elders, so they remained confident they'd made the right decision with Jocelyn Zucklewick, although only time would tell.

If she'd used her attack on Katie to get closer to the students, she would probably be in for a shock. After all, they'd all learnt flight charms as well as the ability to ride on pathways of fire, along with majestic flight astride a Williynx. Also, they'd discovered artefacts which would serve them well in the future, Jacob had explained — their young teacher who kept his cards close to his chest.

Jacob's blossoming romance with Ilina — the girl who'd used a disfigurement charm in The Illustrated Quarter — was an interesting topic to some, especially Leah who had a secret crush on him. She explained her mild obsessions with him as 'general interest', getting looks from the other girls whenever she did. Their teacher was handsome and kind but *off limits*, not that this stopped Leah dreaming.

"I wonder what her first lesson's going to be," Katie said, doing her best to be less domineering.

"A card trick, maybe," Tom quipped, uttering 'Gamas' to do just this, generating cards from the flurry of light appearing around his hands. "A quick game of poker before they arrive."

"How do you know how to play poker?" Ava queried. "You're *twelve*."

"Twelve-and-a-half, actually, which almost makes me a teenager."

"Meaning?"

"Meaning every teenager should learn how to play poker?"

"Why?" Roan queried, thankful Ethan had paused his mock-strangulation.

"Because it's another game of skill and wit. It definitely helps with Rucklz."

"You're always on the losing side," Tilly quipped, her flowing red hair almost reaching her waist.

"Only because you cheated last time."

"I wouldn't say *cheated*," Tilly added, "more like adapted. Can poker teach you that?"

"Poker can teach you lots of things."

"Well, let's give it a go," Ava prompted, jumping down from the windowsill. "My dad fancies himself as a bit of a poker whiz; it would be nice to play him some time."

"Players to their tables!" Tom boomed, using the Acousi charm for effect: a spell allowing you to create any sound of choice.

With that, streaks of light filled the classroom ... multicoloured light flooding from the students' hands, courtesy of their penchants ... ribbons of wonder illuminating the room. As tables and chairs were formed, the classmates sat in a circle, studying Tom who took centre stage.

"So, the art of poker is all in ..."

"The bluff," came a voice that made them all jump, Olin and Leah falling off their seats as Jacob arrived with the woman in question: a teacher immediately drawing suspicion from Tilly. "Poker is about bluffing which will certainly come in handy."

"Told you," Tom whispered as he formed his desk and chair, uttering 'Canvia' to create a vision of silver-blue.

"Morning, class."

"Morning, Sir," The Fateful Eight responded, keeping

their eyes on Jocelyn Zucklewick, the mother who'd wormed her way out of trouble after striking at Katie.

Surprisingly, no resentment marked Katie's face — the girl trying to bury her petulant past.

"I'm sure you all know who this is."

Silence was offered as a response.

"And you're going to offer Jocelyn that same courtesy."

The sight of a Zombul in Jacob's right hand got the students' attention ... the silver artefact punctuated with holes that could release any Society creature. The memory of the Ameedis screeching out of it was enough to jolt the class into action: a synchronised "Morning, Miss" enough to spare them another meeting with a vicious creature.

"Jocelyn, as you know, has been appointed as your second teacher, thanks to Ethan and Katie."

Shrugging at the looks they got, the two classmates hoped they hadn't made a mistake, unable to read their new teacher beyond the nervous smile. They knew all about a certain woman who'd 'gone bad' ... Meyen Grayling who'd got lost in a search for power after hiding something *really bad*. Meyen was Jacob's mother and lived in a secret location, another mystery they hoped their teacher would share one day.

"Nice to meet you all," Jocelyn stated, stepping closer as a flurry of Quij entered through the small holes in the wall ... the delicate, luminous creatures hovering around her. "I'm looking forward to getting to you know you better."

"Have you ever taught before?" Tilly asked, deciding she was done with pleasantries.

"No, not in the formal sense. I taught my daughter some things, just to give her a head start."

"That didn't go to plan did it," Olin whispered, immediately wishing he hadn't as a mind-splitting screech filled the room ... the sight of Jacob opening the lid on the Zombul enough to send the students into defensive shells ... Velinis charms creating bubbles of protection around them as silence became their enemy.

With their hands over their ears, they squinted in pain as the density of the sound increased, until Jacob closed the lid on the silver artefact, placing it in his trouser pocket.

"I won't have rudeness or petulance in the class," he stated, gesturing for the students to return to their desks of light. "Always remember The Orium Circle's decision is final, unless you want to take your grievances up with them, of course. In fact, we could write to Weyen Lyell now, expressing your wish to challenge his decision."

Moving over to the corner of the room, Jacob picked up another silver artefact known as a Scribberal: the communication device used in the S.P.M.A. Anyone want to write the note?"

There were no takers, the Quij moving away from Jocelyn to decorate each student's decks.

"That's what I thought," Jacob added. "Now, find your manners and keep your wits about you. I'm sure you'll be more appreciative by the end of the day."

"Sorry," Olin offered, shaking the brown hair out of his eyes. "I shouldn't have said that about your daughter."

"You're right," Jocelyn replied, stepping forward in a white dress suit that sparkled. "I didn't teach Ellie well enough because she fell at the first hurdle. She and I are *very thankful* for the second chance we've been given."

Ethan and Katie shared a glance at this comment, buoyed by their new teacher's humility: the very thing that had saved her.

"Has Ellie rejoined her class?" Katie asked.

"Yes, Katie although it's going to take time to regain people's trust. Of course, the same goes for me."

"Well, I trust you," Ethan piped up. "I don't think you meant to hurt Katie."

"I didn't."

"Then why did you stun her?" Tilly challenged, still unconvinced by the act of contrition.

"I was desperate, I suppose, sensing the only way back was getting The Orium Circle's attention. It's hard enough to meet them in person at the best of times, so I realised it needed to be the opposite — the worst of times."

"Well, you got what you wanted," Tilly added, holding their new teacher's gaze, wondering what she had up her sleeve.

If bluffing was the art of poker, Jocelyn Zucklewick was a master bluffer, Tilly decided, rapping her fingers on the desk of light to signal annoyance.

"Yes, I did and now it's time to give you what you want: mastery of magic."

"You said you hadn't taught before," Leah piped up, her friendly manner fading.

"Jocelyn is a Society soldier," Jacob explained, placing the Scribberal on Leah's desk to make a point. "I'm sure you all know what Society soldiers are."

"They roam above ground and beyond The Society Sphere," Ethan said in support of their new teacher, "keeping questionable characters in check and battling monsters."

"Have you battled any monsters?" Ava asked, more intrigued all of a sudden.

"The Dexametris," Jocelyn replied matter-of-factly, drawing sighs of awe from the group.

"You fought in *The Caves of Varakel*?" Tom asked, his

mouth hanging open comically, "when the Society army defeated the Dexametris?"

"Jocelyn was right by my side," Jacob added with a smile, "riding on the back of Williynx as Silverbacks stormed the caves, ripping the weak to shreds as we closed in on the fire-breathing monster."

"And your sister and Kaira killed it," Leah added, looking longingly at Jacob.

"That's right, Leah and they were a similar age to you. In fact, Kaira was the same age as you all: twelve."

"Twelve-and-a-half," Tom replied, realising his pedantic touch wasn't appreciated.

"A twelve-year-old had the intuition, foresight and magical movements to defeat a dark creature and a darker wizard."

"Kaira Renn," Olin whispered, remembering the stories he'd read in The Pancithon — the Society library where he spent his evenings.

Unable to sleep from the excitement of magical living, Olin enjoyed the walk to the ground floor of The Cendryll, nodding to the Society stragglers as he made his way down the spiral staircase, deciding which door to go through. Sometimes, he'd stand under the skylight, watching the stars and wondering about the sky realms hidden within them ... the thought of navigating his way there one day sending a fizz of excitement through him.

"Yes, Kaira," Jacob added, "a Society legend who might pay you a visit one day."

"*No way*," Roan uttered, almost falling off his chair.

"He does that when he fancies someone," Ava teased, offering her friend a smile.

"She's out of my league," Roan replied, deciding to make his desk taller for the hell of it.

As it stretched towards the ceiling, the others copied, laughing as they rose like kings and queens in the company of true royalty: legends who had proven their worth time and time again. Now, it was time to bury resentments and open their eyes and ears, because one thing was certain: the ride of their life had just begun.

Buy Book 2

ABOUT THE AUTHOR

I'm the author of the **Kaira Renn** series, **The Fire Witch Chronicles** and **Magic & Misdemeanours,** all set in The Society for the Preservation of Magical Artefacts. (S.P.M.A.)

If you enjoyed the book, please consider **leaving a review on Amazon.**

To receive updates and a chance to win free copies of future titles, sign up to my newsletter **here.**

You can also join my **Facebook group** dedicated the S.P.M.A. universe.

ALSO BY R.A. LINDO

THE S.P.M.A. UNIVERSE

5 books per series

Kaira Renn Series: origin series

The Fire Witch Chronicles: spin-off series one

Magic & Misdemeanours: spin-off series two

Printed in Poland
by Amazon Fulfillment
Poland Sp. z o.o., Wrocław

88294466R00125